HOW HIGH CAN *YOU* FLY?

Fancy a trip (in at least two senses of the word) to Venus?
Then try Fletcher Pratt's ama … *mula.*
But don't toke av … nless
you're heavily i … and
Publishers respec … l the
other stories herei … tion
– and relish an uns … your
armchair.

SPACED OUT is … unearthly drug tales assembled by ace fantasist Michel Parry. For all seekers of Bizarre Best Buys (and who isn't?) it's the Deal of the Year . . .

Also available in Panther Books

Strange Ecstasies (edited by Michel Parry)
Dream Trips (edited by Michel Parry)

Edited by
Michel Parry
(with illustrations by Jim Pitts)

Spaced Out

PANTHER
GRANADA PUBLISHING
London Toronto Sydney New York

Published by Granada Publishing Limited
in Panther Books 1977

ISBN 0 586 04167 2

A Panther Original

Granada Publishing Limited
Frogmore, St Albans, Herts AL2 2NF
and
3 Upper James Street, London W1R 4BP
1221 Avenue of the Americas, New York, NY 10020, USA
117 York Street, Sydney, NSW 2000, Australia
100 Skyway Avenue, Toronto, Ontario, Canada M9W 3A6
Trio City, Coventry Street, Johannesburg 2001, South Africa
CML Centre, Queen & Wyndham, Auckland 1, New Zealand

Made and printed in Great Britain by
Richard Clay (The Chaucer Press) Ltd
Bungay, Suffolk
Set in Linotype Plantin

Contents

CREDITS AND ACKNOWLEDGEMENTS

The Editor wishes to extend his sincere appreciation to the following authors, agents and publishers for permission to reprint copyright material:

Michael Moorcock for *The Deep Fix*, copyright © 1966 by Compact Books.

Leslie Flood and Robert P. Mills for *All the Weed in the World* by Fritz Leiber, copyright © 1960 by HMH Publishing Co. First published in *Playboy*.

Dr. John D. Clark for *The Roger Bacon Formula* by Fletcher Pratt, copyright © 1929 by Ziff-Davis Publishing Company. First published in *Amazing Stories*.

Kirby McCauley for *Smoke of the Snake* by Carl Jacobi, copyright © 1933 by Street & Smith Publications Inc. First published in *Top-Notch*.

Henry Slesar for *Melodramine*, copyright © 1971 by HMH Publishing Company. First published in *Playboy*.

Virginia Kidd and Grania Davis for *My Head's in a Different Place, Now*, copyright © 1973 by Grania Davis. Reprinted from UNIVERSE 2 by permission of Terry Carr.

Virginia Kidd and R. A. Lafferty for *Sky*, copyright © 1972 by R. A. Lafferty. First published in NEW DIMENSIONS 1, edited by Robert Silverberg.

Henry Morrison Inc. for *All of Them Were Empty* by David Gerrold, copyright © 1972 by David Gerrold. Reprinted from WITH MY FINGER IN MY I.

Spaced Out

Introduction

FIRST CAME *STRANGE ECSTASIES.*

Then there was *DREAM TRIPS.*

And now, once more, by popular demand – here's another collection of heads' tales, of weird fantasy stories about weird and fantastic drugs. Not the kind of drugs you can get from your family doctor. Or even from your family dope-dealer. No, these are very special drugs, extraordinary drugs distilled, not from synthesized chemicals or resinous plants but from imagination, pure and uncut. Such drugs as exist only in the minds of our finest literary alchemists.

Michael Moorcock, for example, in his novelette *The Deep Fix*, introduces us to a trip called Mescalin-Andrenol 19 and shares with us a head-space peopled by such bizarre and diverse characters as The Man With No Navel, the Laughing Cavalier and a Vampire in a turtle-neck. R. A. Lafferty turns us on to some dope that takes you higher than a kite – *Sky*-high, in fact. Fletcher Pratt's concoction, Mandragoreum, takes us even higher. Literally out of this world. As does the disturbing stuff to be scored in *All of Them Were Empty* by David Gerrold, one of the best young SF writers to have emerged in recent years. Another promising newcomer is Grania Davis. She serves up some magical mystery mushrooms. Very tasty, too. Only trouble is – they tend to grow on you. Which should suit some getting-back-to-nature-freaks right down to the ground.

Alternatively, Henry Slesar's racy *Melodramine* takes you

right where the action is. Perhaps even a little too close to the action. If that's not your speed either there's always the more sombre traditional Chinese narcotic offered us by veteran fantasy writer Carl Jacobi in *Smoke of the Snake*. The dreams it induces are said to put opium to shame. Sounds great stuff. Just as long as you don't succumb to the temptation of that mysterious fifth pellet . . .

As I have already mentioned, all these drugs exist only in the realms of fiction. They are indisputably imaginary. So far . . . Because events have an astonishing way of catching up with prophetic fantasy writers. A couple of examples . . .

Half a century ago, in a book called *The Sacred Herb*, Edwardian thriller writer Fergus Hume described the properties of 'a grotesque brown root covered with purple leaves, more or less withered.' He claimed that, by smoking it, the user could achieve astral projection and conversation with the Gods. Which sounds very much like some of the wilder claims made today on behalf of marijuana smoking.

And in a story called *The Drug of Dominion* published in 1915, Donovan Bailey forecast the discovery of lysergic acid (LSD) in his description of an imaginary drug he named Malonaine: 'I can take any man, statesman, soldier, witness, merchant off his guard. I can wipe away, with one whiff of Malonaine, all his mental reserves, his precautions, his fears.' In order to test his discovery on unsuspecting humans, the jubilant scientist of the story sets out with an atomizer full of Malonaine and an ample supply of cigarettes soaked in the drug!

For the present however, drugs such as Mandragoreum and Melodramine and Sky can only be read about. But, who knows, maybe one fine day . . .

Until then, here is the mixture as before. The dose is larger this time and the effects weirder than ever. There are uppers and downers, opium-like dreams of dread and delight, narcotic nirvanas and nightmare nadirs. And all the spaces in between.

In Fritz Leiber's *All the Weed in the World* it is someone's burning ambition to get stoned on, yes, all the weed in the world. An enterprising but selfish ambition. And also limited when compared to what imaginative fiction has to offer – not just *All the Weed in the World* but all the most far-out drugs in the whole wide Universe.

Here are eight of them.

Michel Parry

The Deep Fix

MICHAEL MOORCOCK

For William Burroughs, for obvious reasons.

CHAPTER ONE

QUICKENING SOUNDS in the early dusk. Beat of hearts, surge of blood.

Seward turned his head on the bed and looked toward the window. They were coming again. He raised his drug-wasted body and lowered his feet to the floor. He felt nausea sweep up and through him. Dizzily, he stumbled toward the window, parted the blind and stared out over the white ruins.

The sea splashed far away, down by the harbour, and the mob was again rushing through the overgrown streets toward the Research Lab. They were raggedly dressed and raggedly organized, their faces were thin and contorted with madness, but they were numerous.

Seward decided to activate the Towers once more. He walked shakily to the steel-lined room on his left. He reached out a gray, trembling hand and flicked down three switches on a bank of hundreds. Lights blinked on the board above the switches. Seward walked over to the monitor-computer and spoke to it. His voice was harsh, tired and cracking.

'GREEN 9/7–0 Frequency. RED 8/5–B Frequency.' He didn't bother with the other Towers. Two were enough to deal with the mob outside. Two wouldn't harm anybody too badly.

He walked back into the other room and parted the blind again. He saw the mob pause and look toward the roof where the Towers GREEN 9/7 and RED 8/5 were already beginning to spin. Once their gaze had been fixed on the Towers, they couldn't get it away. A few saw their companions look up and these automatically shut their eyes and dropped to the ground. But the others were now held completely rigid.

One by one, then many at a time, those who stared at the Towers began to jerk and thresh, eyes rolling, foaming at the mouth, screaming (he heard their screams faintly) – exhibiting every sign of an advanced epileptic fit.

Seward leaned against the wall feeling sick. Outside, those who'd escaped were crawling round and inching down the street on their bellies. Then, eyes averted from the Towers, they rose to their feet and began to run away through the ruins.

'Saved again,' he thought bitterly.

What was the point? Could he bring himself to go on activating the Towers every time? Wouldn't there come a day when he would let the mob get into the laboratory, search him out, kill him, smash his equipment? He deserved it, after all. The world was in ruins because of him, because of the Towers and the other Hallucinomats which he'd perfected. The mob wanted its revenge. It was fair.

Yet, while he lived, there might be a way of saving something from the wreckage he had made of mankind's minds. The mobs were not seriously hurt by the Towers. It had been the other machines which had created the real damage. Machines like the Paramats, Schizomats, Engramoscopes, even Michelson's Stroboscope Type 8. A range of instruments which had been designed to help the world and had, instead, virtually destroyed civilization.

The memory was all too clear. He wished it wasn't. Having lost track of time almost from the beginning of the disaster, he had no idea how long this had been going on. A year, maybe? His life had become divided into two sections: drug-stimulated working-period; exhausted, troubled, tranquilized sleeping-period. Sometimes, when the mobs saw the inactive Towers and charged toward the laboratory, he had to protect himself. He had learned to sense the coming of a mob. They never came individually. Mob hysteria had become the universal condition of mankind – for all except Seward who had created it.

Hallucinomatics, neural stimulators, mechanical psycho-simulatory devices, hallucinogenic drugs and machines, all had been developed to perfection at the Hampton Research Laboratory under the brilliant direction of Prof. Lee W. Seward (33), psychophysicist extraordinary, one of the youngest pioneers in the field of hallucinogenic research.

Better for the world if he hadn't been, thought Seward wearily as he lowered his worn-out body into the chair and stared at the table full of notebooks and loose sheets of paper on which he'd been working ever since the result of Experiment Restoration.

Experiment Restoration. A fine name. Fine ideals to inspire it. Fine brains to make it. But something had gone wrong.

Originally developed to help in the work of curing mental disorders of all kinds, whether slight or extreme, the Hallucinomats had been an extension on the old hallucinogenic drugs such as CO2, Mescalin and Lysergic Acid derivatives. Their immediate ancestor was the stroboscope and machines like it. The stroboscope, spinning rapidly, flashing brightly colored patterns into the eyes of a subject, often inducing epilepsy or a similar disorder; the research of Burroughs and his followers into the early types of crude hallucinomats, had all helped to contribute to a better understanding of mental disorders.

But, as research continued, so did the incidence of mental illness rise rapidly throughout the world.

The Hampton Research Laboratory and others like it were formed to combat that rise with what had hitherto been considered near-useless experiments in the field of Hallucinomatics. Seward, who had been stressing the potential importance of his chosen field since university, came into his own. He was made Director of the Hampton Lab.

People had earlier thought of Seward as a crank and of the hallucinomats as being at best toys and at worse 'madness machines,' irresponsibly created by a madman.

But psychiatrists specially trained to work with them, had found them invaluable aids to their studies of mental disorders. It had become possible for a trained psychiatrist to induce in himself a temporary state of mental abnormality by use of these machines. Thus he was better able to understand and help his patients. By different methods – light, sound-waves, simulated brain-waves, and so on – the machines created the symptoms of dozens of basic abnormalities and thousands of permutations. They became an essential part of modern psychiatry.

The result: hundreds and hundreds of patients, hitherto virtually incurable, had been cured completely.

But the birth-rate was rising even faster than had been predicted in the middle part of the century. And mental illness rose faster than the birth-rate. Hundreds of cases could be cured. But there were millions to be cured. There was no mass-treatment for mental illness.

Not yet.

Work at the Hampton Research Lab. became a frantic race to get ahead of the increase. Nobody slept much as, in the great big world outside, individual victims of mental illness turned into groups of – the world had only recently forgotten the old word and now remembered it again – *maniacs*.

An overcrowded, over-pressured world, living on its nerves, cracked up.

The majority of people, of course, did not succumb to total madness. But, those who did, became a terrible problem.

Governments, threatened by anarchy, were forced to reinstitute the cruel, old laws in order to combat the threat. All over the world prisons, hospitals, mental homes, institutions of many kinds, all were turned into Bedlams. This hardly solved the problem. Soon, if the rise continued, the sane would be in a minority.

A dark tide of madness, far worse even than that which had swept Europe in the Middle Ages, threatened to submerge civilization.

Work at the Hampton Research Laboratory speeded up and speeded up – and members of the team began to crack. Not all these cases were noticeable to the overworked men who remained sane. They were too busy with their frantic experiments.

Only Lee Seward and a small group of assistants kept going, making increasing use of stimulant-drugs and depressant-drugs to do so.

But, now that Seward thought back, they had not been sane, they had not remained cool and efficient any more than the others. They had seemed to, that was all. Perhaps the drugs had deceived them.

The fact was, they had panicked – though the signs of panic had been hidden, even to themselves, under the disciplined guise of sober thinking.

Their work on tranquilizing machines had not kept up with their perfection of stimulatory devices. This was because they had had to study the reasons for mental abnormalities before they could begin to devise machines for curing them.

Soon, they decided, the whole world would be mad, well before they could perfect their tranquilomatic machines. They could see no way of speeding up this work any more.

Seward was the first to put it to his team. He remembered his words.

'Gentlemen, as you know, our work on hallucinomats for the actual *curing* of mental disorders is going too slowly. There is no sign of our perfecting such machines in the near future. I have an alternative proposal.'

The alternative proposal had been Experiment Restoration.

The title, now Seward thought about it, had been euphemistic. It should have been called Experiment Diversion. The existing hallucinomats would be set up throughout the world and used to induce *passive* disorders in the minds of the greater part of the human race. The co-operation of national governments and World Council was sought and given. The machines were set up secretly at key points all over the globe.

They began to 'send' the depressive symptoms of various disorders. They worked. People became quiet and passive. A large number went into catatonic states. Others – a great many others, who were potentially inclined to melancholia, manic-depression, certain kinds of schizophrenia – committed suicide. Rivers became clogged with corpses, roads awash with the blood and flesh of those who'd thrown themselves in front of cars. Every time a plane or rocket was seen in the sky, people expected to see at least one body come falling from it. Often whole cargoes of people were killed by the suicide of a captain, driver or pilot of a vehicle.

Even Seward had not suspected the extent of the potential suicides. He was shocked. So was his team.

So were the World Council and the national governments. They told Seward and his team to turn off their machines and reverse the damage they had done, as much as possible.

Seward had warned them of the possible result of doing this. He had been ignored. His machines had been confiscated and the World Council had put untrained or ill-trained operators on them. This was one of the last acts of the World Council. It was one of the last rational – however ill-judged – acts the world knew.

The real disaster had come about when the bungling operators that the World Council had chosen set the hallucinomats to send the full effects of the conditions they'd originally been designed to produce. The operators may have been fools – they were probably mad themselves to do what they did. Seward couldn't know. Most of them had been killed by bands of psychopathic murderers who killed their victims by the hundreds in weird and horrible rites which seemed to mirror those of pre-history – or those of the insane South American cultures before the Spaniards.

Chaos had come swiftly – the chaos that now existed.

Seward and his three remaining assistants had protected themselves the only way they could, by erecting the stroboscopic Towers on the roof of the laboratory building. This kept the mobs off. But it did not help their consciences. One by one Seward's assistants had committed suicide.

Only Seward, keeping himself alive on a series of ever-more-potent drugs, somehow retained his sanity. And, he thought ironically, this sanity was only comparative.

A hypodermic syringe lay on the table and beside it a small bottle marked M-A 19 – Mescalin-Andrenol Nineteen –a drug hitherto only tested on animals, never on human beings. But all the other drugs he had used to keep himself going had either run out or now had poor effects. The M-A 19 was his last hope of being able to continue his work on the tranquilomats he needed to perfect, and thus rectify his mistake in the only way he could.

As he reached for the bottle and the hypodermic, he thought coolly that, now he looked back, the whole world had been suffering from insanity well before he had even considered Experiment Restoration. The decision to make the experiment had been just another symptom of the world-disease. Something like it would have happened sooner or later, whether by natural or artificial means. It wasn't really his fault. He had been nothing much more than fate's tool.

But logic didn't help. In a way it *was* his fault. By now, with an efficient team, he might have been able to have constructed a few experimental tranquilomats at least.

'Now I've got to do it alone,' he thought as he pulled up his trouser leg and sought a vein he could use in his clammy, gray flesh. He had long since given up dabbing the area with anaesthetic. He found a blue vein, depressed the plunger of the needle and sat back in his chair to await results.

CHAPTER TWO

THEY CAME suddenly and were drastic.

His brain and body exploded in a torrent of mingled ecstasy and pain which surged through him. Waves of pale light flickered. Rich darkness followed. He rode a ferris-wheel of erupting sensations and emotions. He fell down a never-ending slope of obsidian rock surrounded by clouds of green, purple, yellow, black. The rock vanished, but he continued to fall.

Then there was the smell of disease and corruption in his nostrils, but even that passed and he was standing up.

World of phosphorescence drifting like golden spheres into black night. Green, blue, red explosions. Towers rotate slowly. Towers Advance. Towers Recede. Advance. Recede. Vanish.

Flickering world of phosphorescent tears falling into the timeless, spaceless wastes of Nowhere. World of Misery. World of Antagonism. World of Guilt. Guilt – guilt – guilt . . .

World of hateful wonder.

Heart throbbing, mind thudding, body shuddering as M-A 19 flowed up the infinity of the spine. Shot into back-brain, shot into mid-brain, shot into fore-brain.

EXPLOSION ALL CENTERS!

No-mind – No-body – No-where.

Dying waves of light danced out of his eyes and away through the dark world. Everything was dying. Cells, sinews, nerves, synapses – all crumbling. Tears of light, fading, fading.

Brilliant rockets streaking into the sky, exploding all together and sending their multicolored globes of light – balls on a Xmas Tree – balls on a great tree – x-mass – drifting slowly earthwards.

Ahead of him was a tall, blocky building constructed of

huge chunks of yellowed granite, like a fortress. Black mist swirled around it and across the bleak, horizonless nightscape.

This was no normal hallucinatory experience. Seward felt the ground under his feet, the warm air on his face, the half-familiar smells. He had no doubt that he had entered another world.

But where was it? How had he got here?

Who had brought him here?

The answer might lie in the fortress ahead. He began to walk toward it. Gravity seemed lighter, for he walked with greater ease than normal and was soon standing looking up at the huge green metallic door. He bunched his fist and rapped on it.

Echoes boomed through numerous corridors and were absorbed in the heart of the fortress.

Seward waited as the door was slowly opened.

A man, who so closely resembled the Laughing Cavalier of the painting that he must have modeled his beard and clothes on it, bowed slightly and said:

'Welcome home, Professor Seward. We've been expecting you.'

The bizarrely dressed man stepped aside and allowed him to pass into a dark corridor.

'Expecting me,' said Seward. 'How?'

The Cavalier replied good-humoredly: 'That's not for me to explain. Here we go – through this door and up this corridor.' He opened the door and turned into another corridor and Seward followed him.

They opened innumerable doors and walked along innumerable corridors.

The complexities of the corridors seemed somehow familiar to Seward. He felt disturbed by them, but the possibility of an explanation overrode his qualms and he willingly followed the Laughing Cavalier deeper and deeper into the fortress, through the twists and turns until they arrived at a door which was probably very close to the center of the fortress.

The Cavalier knocked confidently on the door, but spoke deferentially. 'Professor Seward is here at last, sir.'

A light, cultured voice said from the other side of the door: 'Good. Send him in.'

This door opened so slowly that it seemed to Seward that he was watching a film slowed-down to a fraction of its proper speed. When it had opened sufficiently to let him enter, he went into the room beyond. The Cavalier didn't follow him.

It only occurred to him then that he might be in some kind of mental institution, which would explain the fortress-like nature of the building and the man dressed up like the Laughing Cavalier. But, if so, how had he got here – unless he had collapsed and order had been restored sufficiently for someone to have come and collected him. No, the idea was weak.

The room he entered was full of rich, dark colors. Satin screens and hangings obscured much of it. The ceiling was not visible. Neither was the source of the rather dim light. In the center of the room stood a dais, raised perhaps a foot from the floor. On the dais was an old leather armchair.

In the armchair sat a naked man with a cool, blue skin.

He stood up as Seward entered. He smiled charmingly and stepped off the dais, advancing toward Seward with his right hand extended.

'Good to see you, old boy!' he said heartily.

Dazed, Seward clasped the offered hand and felt his whole arm tingle as if it had had a mild electric shock. The man's strange flesh was firm, but seemed to itch under Seward's palm.

The man was short – little over five feet tall. His eyebrows met in the center and his shiny black hair grew to a widow's peak.

Also, he had no navel.

'I'm glad you could get here, Seward,' he said, walking

back to his dais and sitting in the armchair. He rested his head in one hand, his elbow on the arm of the chair.

Seward did not like to appear ungracious, but he was worried and mystified. 'I don't know where this place is,' he said. 'I don't even know how I got here – unless...'

'Ah, yes – the drug. M-A 19, isn't it? That helped, doubtless. We've been trying to get in touch with you for ages, old boy.'

'I've got work to do – back there,' Seward said obsessionally. 'I'm sorry, but I want to get back as soon as I can. What do you want?'

The Man Without A Navel sighed. 'I'm sorry, too, Seward. But we can't let you go yet. There's something I'd like to ask you – a favor. That was why we were hoping you'd come.'

'What's your problem?' Seward's sense of unreality, never very strong here for, in spite of the world's bizarre appearance, it seemed familiar, was growing weaker. If he could help the man and get back to continue his research he would.

'Well,' smiled the Man Without A Navel, 'it's really your problem as much as ours. You see,' he shrugged diffidently, 'we want your world destroyed.'

'What!' Now something was clear, at last. This man and his kind did belong to another world – whether in space, time, or different dimensions – and they were enemies of Earth. 'You can't expect me to help you do that!' He laughed. 'You *are* joking.'

The Man Without A Navel shook his head seriously. 'Afraid not, old boy.'

'That's why you want me here – you've seen the chaos in the world and you want to take advantage of it – you want me to be a – a fifth columnist.'

'Ah, you remember the old term, eh? Yes. I suppose that is what I mean. I want you to be our agent. Those machines of yours could be modified to make those who are left turn against each other even more than at present. Eh?'

'You must be very stupid if you think I'll do that,' Seward said tiredly. 'I can't help you. I'm trying to help *them*.' Was he trapped here for good? He said weakly: 'You've got to let me go back.'

'Not as easy as that, old boy. I – and my friends – want to enter your world, but we can't until you've pumped up your machines to such a pitch that the entire world is maddened and destroys itself, d'you see?'

'Certainly,' exclaimed Seward. 'But I'm having no part of it!'

Again the Man Without A Navel smiled, slowly. 'You'll weaken soon enough, old boy.'

'Don't be so sure,' Seward said defiantly. 'I've had plenty of chances of giving up – back there. I could have weakened. But I didn't.'

'Ah, but you've forgotten the new factor, Seward.'

'What's that?'

'The M-A 19.'

'What do you mean?'

'You'll know soon enough.'

'Look – I want to get out of this place. You can't keep me – there's no point – I won't agree to your plan. Where is this world, anyway?'

'Knowing that depends on you, old boy,' the man's tone was mocking. 'Entirely on you. A lot depends on you, Seward.'

'I know.'

The Man Without A Navel lifted his head and called: 'Brother Sebastian, are you available?' He glanced back at Seward with an ironical smile. 'Brother Sebastian may be of some help.'

Seward saw the wall-hangings on the other side of the room move. Then, from behind a screen on which was painted a weird, surrealistic scene, a tall, cowled figure emerged, face in shadow, hands folded in sleeves. A monk.

'Yes, sir,' said the monk in a cold, malicious voice.

'Brother Sebastian, Professor Seward here is not quite as ready to comply with our wishes as we had hoped. Can you influence him in any way?'

'Possibly, sir.' Now the tone held a note of anticipation.

'Good. Professor Seward, will you go with Brother Sebastian?'

'No.' Seward had thought the room contained only one door—the one he'd entered through. But now there was a chance of there being more doors – other than the one through which the cowled monk had come. The two men didn't seem to hear his negative reply. They remained where they were, not moving. 'No,' he said again, his voice rising. 'What right have you to do this?'

'Rights? A strange question?' The monk chuckled to himself. It was a sound like ice tumbling into a cold glass.

'Yes – rights. You must have some sort of organization here. Therefore you must have a ruler – or government. I demand to be taken to someone in authority.'

'But I am in authority here, old boy,' purred the blue-skinned man. 'And – in a sense – so are you. If you agreed with my suggestion, you could hold tremendous power. Tremendous.'

'I don't want to discuss that again.' Seward began to walk toward the wall-hangings. They merely watched him – the monk with his face in shadow – the Man Without A Navel with a supercilious smile on his thin lips. He walked around a screen, parted the hangings – and there they were on the other side. He went through the hangings. This was some carefully planned trick – an illusion – deliberately intended to confuse him. He was used to such methods, even though he didn't understand how they'd worked this one.

He said: 'Clever – but tricks of this kind won't make me weaken.'

'What on earth d'you mean, Seward, old man? Now, I wonder if you'll accompany Brother Sebastian here. I have an awful lot of work to catch up on.'

'All right,' Seward said. 'All right, I will.' Perhaps on the way to wherever the monk was going, he would find an opportunity to escape.

The monk turned and Seward followed him. He did not look at the Man Without A Navel as he passed his ridiculous dais, with its ridiculous leather armchair.

They passed through a narrow doorway behind a curtain and were once again in the complex series of passages. The tall monk – now he was close to him, Seward estimated his height at about six feet, seven inches – seemed to flow along in front of him. He began to dawdle. The monk didn't look back. Seward increased the distance between them. Still, the monk didn't appear to notice.

Seward turned and ran.

They had met nobody on their journey through the corridors. He hoped he could find a door leading out of the fortress before someone spotted him. There was no cry from behind him.

But as he ran, the passages got darker and darker until he was careering through pitch blackness, sweating, panting and beginning to panic. He kept blundering into damp walls and running on.

It was only much later that he began to realize he was running in a circle that was getting tighter and tighter until he was doing little more than spin round, like a top. He stopped, then.

These people evidently had more powers than he had suspected. Possibly they had some means of shifting the position of the corridor walls, following his movements by means of hidden TV cameras or something like them. Simply because there were no visible signs of an advanced technology didn't mean that they did not possess one. They obviously did. How else could they have got him from his own world to this?

He took a pace forward. Did he sense the walls drawing back? He wasn't sure. The whole thing reminded him vaguely of *The Pit and The Pendulum.*

He strode forward a number of paces and saw a light ahead of him. He walked toward it, turned into a dimly-lit corridor.

The monk was waiting for him.

'We missed each other, Professor Seward. I see you managed to precede me.' The monk's face was still invisible, secret in its cowl. As secret as his cold, mocking, malevolent voice. 'We are almost there, now,' said the monk.

Seward stepped toward him, hoping to see his face, but it was impossible. The monk glided past him. 'Follow me, please.'

For the moment, until he could work out how the fortress worked, Seward decided to accompany the monk.

They came to a heavy, iron-studded door – quite unlike any of the other doors.

They walked into a low-ceilinged chamber. It was very hot. Smoke hung in the still air of the room. It poured from a glowing brazier at the extreme end. Two men stood by the brazier.

One of them was a thin man with a huge, bulging stomach over which his long, narrow hands were folded. He had a shaggy mane of dirty white hair, his cheeks were sunken and his nose extremely long and extremely pointed. He seemed toothless and his puckered lips were shaped in a senseless smile – like the smile of a madman Seward had once had to experiment on. He wore a stained white jacket buttoned over his grotesque paunch. On his legs were loose khaki trousers.

His companion was also thin, though lacking the stomach. He was taller and had the face of a mournful bloodhound, with sparse, highly-greased, black hair that covered his bony head like a skull-cap. He stared into the brazier, not looking up as Brother Sebastian led Seward into the room and closed the door.

The thin man with the stomach, however, pranced forward, his hands still clasped on his paunch, and bowed to them both.

'Work for us, Brother Sebastian?' he said, nodding at Seward.

'We require a straightforward "Yes,"' Brother Sebastian

said. 'You have merely to ask the question "Will you?" If he replies "No," you are to continue. If he replies "Yes," you are to cease and inform me immediately.'

'Very well, Brother. Rely on us.'

'I hope I can.' The monk chuckled again. 'You are now in the charge of these men, professor. If you decide you want to help us, after all, you have only to say "Yes." Is that clear?'

Seward began to tremble with horror. He had suddenly realized what this place was.

'Now look here,' he said. 'You can't . . .'

He walked toward the monk who had turned and was opening the door. He grasped the man's shoulder. His hand seemed to clutch a delicate, bird-like structure. 'Hey! I don't think you're a man at all. What *are* you?'

'A man or a mouse,' chuckled the monk as the two grotesque creatures leapt forward suddenly and twisted Seward's arms behind him. Seward kicked back at them with his heels, squirmed in their grasp, but he might have been held by steel bands. He shouted incoherently at the monk as he shut the door behind him with a whisk of his habit.

The pair flung him on to the damp, hot stones of the floor. It smelt awful. He rolled over and sat up. They stood over him. The hound-faced man had his arms folded. The thin man with the stomach had his long hands on his paunch again. They seemed to rest there whenever he was not actually using them. It was the latter who smiled with his twisting, puckered lips, cocking his head to one side.

'What do *you* think, Mr. Morl?' he asked his companion.

'I don't know, Mr. Hand. After you.' The hound-faced man spoke in a melancholy whisper.

'I would suggest Treatment H. Simple to operate, less work for us, a tried and trusty operation which works with most and will probably work with this gentleman.'

Seward scrambled up and tried to push past them, making for the door. Again they seized him expertly and dragged him back. He felt the rough touch of rope on his wrists and the pain as a knot was tightened. He shouted, more in anger than agony, more in terror than either.

They were going to torture him. He knew it.

When they had tied his hands, they took the rope and tied his ankles. They twisted the rope up around his calves and under his legs. They made a halter of the rest and looped it over his neck so that he had to bend almost double if he was not to strangle.

Then they sat him on a chair.

Mr. Hand removed his hands from his paunch, reached up above Seward's head and turned on the tap.

The first drop of water fell directly on the center of his head some five minutes later.

Twenty-seven drops of water later, Seward was raving and screaming. Yet every time he tried to jerk his head away, the halter threatened to strangle him and the jolly Mr. Hand and the mournful Mr. Morl were there to straighten him up again.

Thirty drops of water after that, Seward's brain began to throb and he opened his eyes to see that the chamber had vanished.

In its place was a huge comet, a fireball dominating the sky, rushing directly toward him. He backed away from it and there were no more ropes on his hands or feet. He was free.

He began to run. He leapt into the air and stayed there. He was swimming through the air.

Ecstasy ran up his spine like a flickering fire, touched his back-brain, touched his mid-brain, touched his fore-brain.

EXPLOSION ALL CENTERS!

He was standing, one flower among many, in a bed of tall lupins and roses which waved in a gentle wind. He pulled his roots free and began to walk.

He walked into the Lab Control Room.

Everything was normal except that gravity seemed a little heavy. Everything was as he'd left it.

He saw that he had left the Towers rotating. He went into the room he used as a bedroom and workroom. He parted the blind and looked out into the night. There was a big, full moon hanging in the deep, blue sky over the ruins of Hampton. He saw its light reflected in the faraway sea. A few bodies still lay prone near the lab. He went back into the Control Room and switched off the Towers.

Returning to the bedroom he looked at the card-table he had his notes on. They were undisturbed. Neatly, side by side near a large, tattered notebook, lay a half-full ampoule of M-A 19 and a hypodermic syringe. He picked up the ampoule and threw it in a corner. It did not break but rolled around on the floor for a few seconds.

He sat down.

His whole body ached.

He picked up a sheaf of his more recent notes. He wrote everything down that came into his head on the subject of tranquilomats; it helped him think better and made sure that his drugged mind and body did not hamper him as much as they might have done if he had simply relied on his memory.

He looked at his wrists. They carried the marks of the rope. Evidently the transition from the other world to his own involved leaving anything in the other world behind. He was glad. If he hadn't, he'd have had a hell of a job getting himself untied. He shuddered – a mob might have reached the lab before he could get free and activate the Towers.

He tried hard to forget the questions flooding through his mind. Where had he been? Who were the people? What did they really want? How far could they keep a check on him? How did the M-A 19 work to aid his transport into the other world? Could they get at him here?

He decided they couldn't get at him, otherwise they might have tried earlier. Somehow it was the M-A 19 in his brain which allowed them to get hold of him. Well, that was simple – no more M-A 19.

With a feeling of relief, he forced himself to concentrate on his notes.

Out of the confusion, something seemed to be developing, but he had to work at great speed – greater speed than previously, perhaps, for he daren't use the M-A 19 again and there was nothing else left of much good.

His brain cleared as he once again got interested in his notes. He worked for two hours, making fresh notes, equations, checking his knowledge against the stack of earlier research notes by the wall near his camp bed.

Dawn was coming as he realized suddenly that he was suffering from thirst. His throat was bone dry, so were his mouth and lips. He got up and his legs felt weak. He staggered, almost knocking over the chair. With a great effort he righted it and, leaning for support on the bed, got himself to the hand-basin. It was filled by a tank near the roof and he had used it sparsely. But this time he didn't care. He stuck his head under the tap and drank the stale water greedily. It did no good. His whole body now seemed cold, his skin tight, his heart thumping heavily against his ribs. His head was aching horribly and his breathing increased.

He went and lay down on the bed, hoping the feeling would leave him.

It got worse. He needed something to cure himself.

What? he asked.

M-A 19, he answered.

No!

But — Yes, yes, yes. All he needed was a small shot of the drug and he would be all right. He knew it.

And with knowing that, he realized something else.

He was hooked.

The drug was habit-forming.

CHAPTER THREE

He found the half-full M-A ampoule under the bed where it had rolled. He found the needle on the table where he had left it, buried under his notes. He found a vein in his forearm and shot himself full. There was no thought to Seward's action. There was just craving and the chance of satisfying that craving.

The M-A 19 began to swim leisurely through his veins, drifting up his spine —

It hit his brain with a powerful explosion.

He was walking through a world of phosphorescent rain, leaping over large purple rocks that welcomed his feet, drew them down toward them. All was agony and startling Now.

No-time, no-space, just the throbbing voice in the air above him. It was talking to him.

DOOM, Seward. DOOM, Seward. DOOM, Seward.

'Seward is doomed!' he laughed. 'Seward is betrayed!'

Towers Advance. Towers Recede. Towers Rotate At Normal Speed.

Carnival Aktion. All Carnivals To Explode.

Up into the back-brain, into the mid-brain, on to the fore-brain.

EXPLOSION ALL CENTERS!

He was back in the torture-chamber, though standing up. In the corner near the brazier the grotesque pair were muttering to each other. Mr. Hand darted him an angry glance, his lips drawn over his gums in an expression of outrage.

'Hello, Seward,' said the Man Without A Navel behind him. 'So you're back.'

'Back,' said Seward heavily. 'What more do you want?'

'Only your All, Seward, old man. I remember a time in Dartford before the War . . .'

'Which war?'

'Your war, Seward. You were too young to share any other.

You don't remember *that* war. You weren't born. Leave it to those who do, Seward.'

Seward turned. 'My war?' He looked with disgust at the Man Without A Navel; at his reptilian blue skin and his warm-cold, dark-light, good-evil eyes. At his small well-formed body.

The Man Without A Navel smiled. '*Our* war, then, old man. I won't quibble.'

'You made me do it. I think that somehow you made me suggest Experiment Restoration!'

'I said we won't quibble, Seward,' said the man in an authoritative tone. Then, more conversationally: 'I remember a time in Dartford before the War, when you sat in your arm-chair – one rather like mine – at your brother-in-law's house. Remember what you said, old man?'

Seward remembered well. 'If,' he quoted, 'if I had a button and could press it and destroy the entire universe and myself with it, I would. For no reason other than boredom.'

'Very good, Seward. You have an excellent memory.'

'Is that all you're going on? Something I said out of frustration because nobody was recognizing my work?' He paused as he realized something else. 'You know all about me, don't you?' he said bitterly. There seemed to be nothing he didn't know. On the other hand Seward knew nothing of the man. Nothing of this world. Nothing of where it was in space and time. It was a world of insanity, of bizarre contrasts. '*How* do you know all this?'

'Inside information, Seward, old boy.'

'You're mad!'

The Man Without A Navel returned to his earlier topic. 'Are you bored now, Seward?'

'Bored? No. Tired, yes.'

'Bored, no – tired, yes. Very good, Seward. You got here later than expected. What kept you?' The man laughed.

'I kept me. I held off taking the M-A 19 for as long as I could.'

'But you came to us in the end, eh? Good man, Seward.'

'You knew the M-A 19 was habit-forming? You knew I'd have to take it, come back here?'

'Naturally.'

He said pleadingly: 'Let me go for God's sake! You've made me. Made me . . .'

'Your dearest wish almost come true, Seward. Isn't that what you wanted? I made you come close to destroying the world? Is that it?'

'So you did somehow influence Experiment Restoration!'

'It's possible. But you haven't done very well either way. The world is in shambles. You can't reverse that. Kill it off. Let's start fresh, Seward. Forget your experiments with the tranquilomats and help us.'

'No.'

The Man Without A Navel shrugged. 'We'll see, old boy.'

He looked at the mumbling men in the corner. 'Morl – Hand – take Professor Seward to his room. I don't want any mistakes this time. I'm going to take him out of your hands. Obviously we need subtler minds put on the problem.'

The pair came forward and grabbed Seward. The Man Without A Navel opened the door and they went through it first, forcing Seward ahead of them.

He was too demoralized to resist much, this time. Demoralized by the fact that he was hooked on M-A 19. What did the Junkies call it? The Habit. He had The Habit. Demoralized by his inability to understand the whereabouts or nature of the world he was on. Demoralized by the fact that the Man Without A Navel seemed to know everything about his personal life on Earth. Demoralized that he had fallen into the man's trap. Who had developed M-A 19? He couldn't remember. Perhaps the Man Without A Navel had planted it? He supposed it might be possible.

He was pushed along another series of corridors, arrived at another door. The Man Without A Navel came up behind them and unlocked the door.

Seward was shoved into the room. It was narrow and low – coffin-like.

'We'll be sending someone along to see you in a little while, Seward,' said the man lightly. The door was slammed.

Seward lay in pitch blackness.

He began to sob.

Later, he heard a noise outside. A stealthy noise of creeping feet. He shuddered. What was the torture going to be this time?

He heard a scraping and a muffled rattle. The door opened.

Against the light from the passage, Seward saw the man clearly. He was a big, fat Negro in a gray suit. He wore a flowing, rainbow-colored tie. He was grinning.

Seward liked the man instinctively. But he no longer trusted his instinct. 'What do you want?' he said suspiciously.

The huge Negro raised his finger to his lips. 'Ssshh,' he whispered. 'I'm going to try and get you out of here.'

'An old Secret Police trick on my world,' said Seward. 'I'm not falling for that.'

'It's no trick, son. Even if it is, what can you lose?'

'Nothing.' Seward got up.

The big man put his arm round Seward's shoulders. Seward felt comfortable in the grip, though normally he disliked such gestures.

'Now, son, we go real quietly and we go as fast as we can. Come on.'

Softly, the big man began to tiptoe along the corridor. Seward was sure that TV cameras, or whatever they were, were following him, that the Man Without A Navel, the monk, the two torturers, the Laughing Cavalier, were all waiting somewhere to seize him.

But, very quickly, the Negro had reached a small wooden door and was drawing a bolt. He patted Seward's shoulder and held the door open for him. 'Through you go, son. Make for the red car.'

It was morning. In the sky hung a golden sun, twice the

size of Earth's. There was a vast expanse of lifeless rock in all directions, broken only by a white road which stretched into the distance. On the road, close to Seward, was parked a car something like a Cadillac. It was fire-red and bore the registration plates YOU 000. Whoever these people were, Seward decided, they were originally from Earth – all except the Man Without A Navel, perhaps. Possibly this was his world and the others had been brought from Earth, like him.

He walked toward the car. The air was cold and fresh. He stood by the convertible and looked back. The Negro was running over the rock toward him. He dashed round the car and got into the driver's seat. Seward got in beside him.

The Negro started the car, put it into gear and shoved his foot down hard on the accelerator pedal. The car jerked away and had reached top speed in seconds.

At the wheel, the Negro relaxed. 'Glad that went smoothly. I didn't expect to get away with it so easily, son. You're Seward, aren't you?'

'Yes. You seem to be as well-informed as the others.'

'I guess so.' The Negro took a pack of cigarettes from his shirt pocket. 'Smoke?'

'No thanks,' said Seward. 'That's one habit I don't have.'

The Negro looked back over his shoulder. The expanse of rock seemed never-ending, though in the distance the fortress was disappearing. He flipped a cigarette out of the pack and put it between his lips. He unclipped the car's lighter and put it to the tip of the cigarette. He inhaled and put the lighter back. The cigarette between his lips, he returned the other hand to the wheel.

He said: 'They were going to send the Vampire to you. It's lucky I reached you in time.'

'It could be,' said Seward. 'Who are you? What part do you play in this?'

'Let's just say I'm a friend of yours and an enemy of your enemies. The name's Farlowe.'

'Well, I trust you, Farlowe – though God knows why.'

Farlowe grinned. 'Why not? I don't want your world destroyed any more than you do. It doesn't much matter, I guess, but if there's a chance of restoring it, then you ought to try.'

'Then you're from my world originally, is that it?'

'In a manner of speaking, son,' said Farlowe.

Very much later, the rock gave way to pleasant, flat countryside with trees, fields and little cottages peaceful under the vast sky. In the distance, Seward saw herds of cattle and sheep, the occasional horse. It reminded him of the countryside of his childhood, all clear and fresh and sharp with the clarity that only a child's eye can bring to a scene before it is obscured and tainted by the impressions of adulthood. Soon the flat country was behind them and they were going through an area of low, green hills, the huge sun flooding the scene with its soft, golden light. There were no clouds in the pale blue sky.

The big car sped smoothly along and Seward, in the comfortable companionship of Farlowe, began to relax a little. He felt almost happy, would have felt happy if it had not been for the nagging knowledge that somehow he had to get back and continue his work. It was not merely a question of restoring sanity to the world, now – he had also to thwart whatever plans were in the mind of the Man Without A Navel.

After a long silence, Seward asked a direct question. 'Farlowe, where is this world? What are we doing here?'

Farlowe's answer was vague. He stared ahead at the road. 'Don't ask me that, son. I don't rightly know.'

'But you live here.'

'So do you.'

'No – I only come here when – when ...'

'When what?'

But Seward couldn't raise the courage to admit about the drug to Farlowe. Instead he said: 'Does M-A 19 mean anything to you?'

'Nope.'

So Farlowe hadn't come here because of the drug. Seward said: 'But you said you were from my world originally.'

'Only in a manner of speaking.' Farlowe changed gears as the road curved steeply up a hill. It rose gently above the idyllic countryside below.

Seward changed his line of questioning. 'Isn't there any sort of organization here – no government? What's the name of this country?'

Farlowe shrugged. 'It's just a place – no government. The people in the fortress run most things. Everybody's scared of them.'

'I don't blame them. Who's the Vampire you mentioned?'

'He works for the Man.'

'What is he?'

'Why – a vampire, naturally,' said Farlowe in surprise.

The sun had started to set and the whole countryside was bathed in red-gold light. The car continued to climb the long hill.

Farlowe said: 'I'm taking you to some friends. You ought to be fairly safe there. Then maybe we can work out a way of getting you back.'

Seward felt better. At least Farlowe had given him some direct information.

As the car reached the top of the hill and began to descend Seward got a view of an odd and disturbing sight. The sun was like a flat, round, red disc – yet only half of it was above the horizon. *The line of the horizon evenly intersected the sun's disc!* It was some sort of mirage – yet so convincing that Seward looked away, staring instead at the black smoke which he could now see rolling across the valley below. He said nothing to Farlowe.

'How much further?' he asked later as the car came to the bottom of the hill. Black night had come, moonless, and the car's headlights blazed.

'A long way yet, I'm afraid, son,' said Farlowe. 'You cold?'

'No.'

'We'll be hitting a few signs of civilization soon. You tired?'

'No – why?'

'We could put up at a motel or something. I guess we could eat anyway.'

Ahead, Seward saw a few lights. He couldn't make out where they came from. Farlowe began to slow down. 'We'll risk it,' he said. He pulled in toward the lights and Seward saw that it was a line of fuel pumps. Behind the pumps was a single-story building, very long and built entirely of timber by the look of it. Farlowe drove in between the pumps and the building. A man in overalls, the top half of his face shadowed by the peak of his cap, came into sight. Farlowe got out of the car with a signal to Seward to do the same. The Negro handed his keys to the attendant. 'Fill her full and give her a quick check.'

Could this be Earth? Seward wondered. Earth in the future – or possibly an Earth of a different space-time continuum? That was the likeliest explanation for this unlikely world. The contrast between recognizable, everyday things and the grotesqueries of the fortress was strange – yet it could be explained easily if these people had contact with his world. That would explain how they had things like cars and fuel stations and no apparent organizations necessary for producing them. Somehow, perhaps, they just – *stole* them?

He followed Farlowe into the long building. He could see through the wide windows that it was some kind of restaurant. There was a long, clean counter and a few people seated at tables at the far end. All had their backs to him.

He and Farlowe sat down on stools. Close to them was the largest pin-table Seward had ever seen. Its lights were flashing and its balls were clattering, though there was no one operating it. The colored lights flashed series of numbers at him until his eyes lost focus and he had to turn away.

A woman was standing behind the counter now. Most of her face was covered by a yashmak.

'What do you want to eat, son?' said Farlowe, turning to him.

'Oh, anything.'

Farlowe ordered sandwiches and coffee. When the woman had gone to get their order, Seward whispered: 'Why's she wearing that thing?'

Farlowe pointed at a sign Seward hadn't noticed before. It read THE HAREM HAVEN. 'It's their gimmick,' said Farlowe.

Seward looked back at the pin-table. The lights had stopped flashing, the balls had stopped clattering. But above it suddenly appeared a huge pair of disembodied eyes. He gasped.

Distantly, he heard his name being repeated over and over again. 'Seward. Seward. Seward. Seward . . .'

He couldn't tell where the voice was coming from. He glanced up at the ceiling. Not from there. The voice stopped. He looked back at the pin-table. The eyes had vanished. His panic returned. He got off his stool.

'I'll wait for you in the car, Farlowe.'

Farlowe looked surprised. 'What's the matter, son?'

'Nothing – it's okay – I'll wait in the car.'

Farlowe shrugged.

Seward went out into the night. The attendant had gone but the car was waiting for him. He opened the door and climbed in.

What did the eyes mean? Were the people from the fortress following him in some way? Suddenly an explanation for most of the questions bothering him sprang into his mind. Of course – telepathy. They were probably telepaths. That was how they knew so much about him. That could be how they knew of his world and could influence events there – they might never go there in person. This comforted him a little, though he realized that getting out of this situation was going to be even more difficult than he'd thought.

He looked through the windows and saw Farlowe's big body perched on its stool. The other people in the café were still sitting with their backs to him. He realized that there was something familiar about them.

He saw Farlowe get up and walk towards the door. He came out and got into the car, slamming the door after him. He leaned back into his seat and handed Seward a sandwich. 'You seem worked up, son,' he said. 'You'd better eat this.'

Seward took the sandwich. He was staring at the backs of the other customers again. He frowned.

Farlowe started the car and they moved toward the road. Then Seward realized who the men reminded him of. He craned his head back in the hope of seeing their faces, but it was too late. They had reminded him of his dead assistants – the men who'd committed suicide.

They roared through dimly-seen towns – all towers and angles. There seemed to be nobody about. Dawn came up and they still sped on. Seward realized that Farlowe must have a tremendous vitality, for he didn't seem to tire at all. Also, perhaps, he was motivated by a desire to get as far away from the fortress as possible.

They stopped twice to refuel and Farlowe bought more sandwiches and coffee which they had as they drove.

In the late afternoon Farlowe said: 'Almost there.'

They passed through a pleasant village. It was somehow alien, although very similar to a small English village. It had an oddly foreign look which was hard to place. Farlowe pulled in at what seemed to be the gates of a large public park. He looked up at the sun. 'Just made it,' he said. 'Wait in the park – someone will come to collect you.'

'You're leaving me?'

'Yes. I don't think they know where you are. They'll look but, with luck, they won't look around here. Out you get, son. Into the park.'

'Who do I wait for?'

'You'll know her when she comes.'

'Her?' He got out and closed the door. He stood on the pavement watching as, with a cheerful wave, Farlowe drove off. He felt a tremendous sense of loss then, as if his only hope had been taken away.

Gloomily, he turned and walked through the park gates.

CHAPTER FOUR

As HE walked between low hedges along a gravel path, he realized that this park, like so many things in this world, contrasted with the village it served. It was completely familiar just like a park on his own world.

It was a gray, hazy winter's afternoon, with the brittle, interwoven skeletons of trees black and sharp against the cold sky. Birds perched on trees and bushes, or flew noisily into the silent air.

Evergreens crowded upon the leaf-strewn grass. Cry of sparrows. Peacocks, necks craned forward, dived toward scattered bread. Silver birch, larch, elm, monkey-puzzle trees, and swaying white ferns, each one like an ostrich feather stuck in the earth. A huge, ancient, nameless trunk from which, at the top, grew an expanse of soft, yellow fungus; the trunk itself looking like a Gothic cliff, full of caves and dark windows. A gray and brown pigeon perched motionless on the slender branches of a young birch. Peacock chicks the size of hens pecked with concentration at the grass.

Mellow, nostalgic smell of winter; distant sounds of children playing; lost black dog looking for master; red disc of sun in the cool, darkening sky. The light was sharp and yet soft, peaceful. A path led into the distance toward a flight of wide stone steps, at the top of which was the curving entrance to an arbor, browns, blacks and yellows of sapless branches and fading leaves.

From the arbor a girl appeared and began to descend the steps with quick, graceful movements. She stopped when she reached the path. She looked at him. She had long, blonde hair and wore a white dress with a full skirt. She was about seventeen.

The peace of the park was suddenly interrupted by children rushing from nowhere toward the peacocks, laughing and shouting. Some of the boys saw the tree trunk and made for it. Others stood looking upward at the sun as it sank in the cold air. They seemed not to see either Seward or the girl. Seward looked at her. Did he recognize her? It wasn't possible. Yet she, too, gave him a look of recognition, smiled shyly at him and ran toward him. She reached him, stood on tiptoe and gave him a light kiss on the cheek.

'Hello, Lee.'

'Hello. Have you come to find me?'

'I've been looking for you a long time.'

'Farlowe sent a message ahead?'

She took his hand. 'Come on. Where have you been, Lee?'

This was a question he couldn't answer. He let her lead him back up the steps, through the arbor. Between the branches he glanced at a garden and a pool. 'Come on,' she said. 'Let's see what's for dinner. Mother's looking forward to meeting you.'

He no longer questioned how these strange people all seemed to know his name. It was still possible that all of them were taking part in the conspiracy against him.

At the end of the arbor was a house, several stories high. It was a pleasant house with a blue and white door. She led him up the path and into a hallway. It was shining with dark polished wood and brass plates on the walls. From a room at the end he smelled spicy cooking. She went first and opened the door at the end. 'Mother – Lee Seward's here. Can we come in?'

'Of course.' The voice was warm, husky, full of humor. They went into the room and Seward saw a woman of about forty, very well-preserved, tall, large-boned with a fine-featured face and smiling mouth. Her eyes also smiled. Her sleeves were rolled up and she put the lid back on a pan on the stove.

'How do you do, Professor Seward. Mr. Farlowe's told us about you. You're in trouble, I hear.'

'How do you do, Mrs. —'

'Call me Martha. Has Sally introduced herself?'

'No,' Sally laughed. 'I forgot. I'm Sally, Lee.'

Her mother gave a mock frown. 'I suppose you've been calling our guest by his first name, as usual. Do you mind, professor?'

'Not at all.' He was thinking how attractive they both were, in their different ways. The young, fresh girl and her warm, intelligent mother. He had always enjoyed the company of women, but never so much, he realized, as now. They seemed to complement one another. In their presence he felt safe, at ease. Now he realized why Farlowe had chosen them to hide him. Whatever the facts, he would feel safe here.

Martha was saying: 'Dinner won't be long.'

'It smells good.'

'Probably smells better than it tastes,' she laughed. 'Go into the lounge with Sally. Sally, fix Professor Seward a drink.'

'Call me Lee,' said Seward, a little uncomfortably. He had never cared much for his first name. He preferred his middle name, William, but not many others did.

'Come on, Lee.' She took his hand and led him out of the kitchen. 'We'll see what there is.' They went into a small, well-lighted lounge. The furniture, like the whole house, had a look that was half-familiar, half-alien – obviously the product of a slightly different race. Perhaps they deliberately imitated Earth culture, without quite succeeding. Sally still gripped his hand. Her hand was warm and her skin smooth. He made to drop it but, involuntarily, squeezed it gently before she took it away to deal with the drink. She gave him another shy smile. He felt that she was as attracted to him as he to her. 'What's it going to be?' she asked him.

'Oh, anything,' he said, sitting down on a comfortable sofa. She poured him a dry martini and brought it over. Then demurely she sat down beside him and watched him drink it. Her eyes sparkled with a mixture of sauciness and innocence which he found extremely appealing. He looked around the room.

'How did Farlowe get his message to you?' he said

'He came the other day. Said he was going to try and get into the fortress and help you. Farlowe's always flitting about. I think the people at the fortress have a price on his head or something. It's exciting, isn't it?'

'You can say that again,' Seward said feelingly.

'Why are they after you?'

'They want me to help them destroy the world I come from. Do you know anything about it?'

'Earth, isn't it?'

'Yes.' Was he going to get some straightforward answers at last?

'I know it's very closely connected with ours and that some of us want to escape from here and go to your world.'

'Why?' he asked eagerly.

She shook her head. Her long, fine hair waved with the motion. 'I don't really know. Something about their being trapped here – something like that. Farlowe said something about you being a "key" to their release. They can only do what they want to do with your agreement.'

'But I could agree and then break my word!'

'I don't think you could – but honestly, I don't know any more. I've probably got it wrong. Do you like me, Lee?'

He was startled by the directness of her question. 'Yes,' he said, 'very much.'

'Farlowe said you would. Good, isn't it?'

'Why – yes. Farlowe knows a lot.'

'That's why he works against *them*.'

Martha came in. 'Almost ready,' she smiled. 'I think I'll have a quick one before I start serving. How are you feeling, Lee, after your ride?'

'Fine,' he said, 'fine.' He had never been in a position like this one – with two women either of whom was extremely attractive for almost opposite reasons.

'We were discussing why the people at the fortress wanted

my help,' he said, turning the conversation back the way he felt it ought to go if he was ever going to get off this world and back to his own and his work.

'Farlowe said something about it.'

'Yes, Sally told me. Does Farlowe belong to some sort of underground organization?'

'Underground? Why, yes, in a way he does.'

'Aren't they strong enough to fight the Man Without A Navel and his friends?'

'Farlowe said they're strong enough, but divided over what should be done and how.'

'I see. That's fairly common amongst such groups, I believe.'

'Yes.'

'What part do you play?'

'None, really. Farlowe asked me to put you up – that's all.' She sipped her drink, her eyes smiling directly into his. He drained his glass.

'Shall we eat?' she said. 'Sally, take Lee in to the dining room.'

The girl got up and, somewhat possessively, Seward thought, linked her arm in his. Her young body against his was distracting. He felt a little warm. She took him in. The table was laid for supper. Three chairs and three places. The sun had set and candles burned on the table in brass candelabra. She unlinked her arm and pulled out one of the chairs.

'You sit here, Lee – at the head of the table.' She grinned. Then she leaned forward as he sat down. 'Hope mummy isn't boring you.'

He was surprised. 'Why should she?'

Martha came in with three covered dishes on a tray. 'This may not have turned out quite right, Lee. Never does when you're trying hard.'

'I'm sure it'll be fine,' he smiled. The two women sat down one either side of him. Martha served him. It was some sort of goulash with vegetables. He took his napkin and put it on his lap.

As they began to eat, Martha said: 'How is it?'

'Fine,' he said. It was very good. Apart from the feeling that some kind of rivalry for his attentions existed between mother and daughter the air of normality in the house was comforting. Here, he might be able to do some constructive thinking about his predicament.

When the meal was over, Martha said: 'It's time for bed, Sally. Say good night to Lee.'

She pouted. 'Oh, it's not fair.'

'Yes it is,' she said firmly. 'You can see Lee in the morning. He's had a long journey.'

'All right.' She smiled at Seward. 'Sleep well, Lee.'

'I think I will,' he said.

Martha chuckled after Sally had gone. 'Would you like a drink before you go to bed?' She spoke softly.

'Love one,' he said.

They went into the other room. He sat down on the sofa as she mixed the drinks. She brought them over and sat down next to him as her daughter had done earlier.

'Tell me everything that's been happening. It sounds so exciting.'

He knew at once he could tell her all he wanted to, that she would listen and be sympathetic. 'It's terrifying, really,' he began, half-apologetically. He began to talk, beginning with what had happened on Earth. She listened.

'I even wondered if this was a dream-world – a figment of my imagination,' he finished, 'but I had to reject that when I went back to my own. I had rope marks on my wrists – my hair was soaking wet. You don't get that in a dream!'

'I hope not,' she smiled. 'We're different here, Lee, obviously. Our life doesn't have the – the *shape* that yours has. We haven't much direction, no real desires. We just – well – *exist*. It's as if we're waiting for something to happen. As if —' she paused and seemed to be looking down deep into herself. 'Put it this way – Farlowe thinks you're the key figure in some development that's happening here. Supposing

– supposing we were some kind of – of experiment . . .'

'Experiment? How do you mean?'

'Well, from what you say, the people at the fortress have an advanced science that we don't know about. Supposing our parents, say, had been kidnapped from your world and – made to think – what's the word —'

'Conditioned?'

'Yes, conditioned to think they were natives of this world. We'd have grown up knowing nothing different. Maybe the Man Without A Navel is a member of an alien race – a scientist of some kind in charge of the experiment.'

'But why should they make such a complicated experiment?'

'So they could study us, I suppose.'

Seward marveled at her deductive powers. She had come to a much firmer theory than he had. But then, he thought, she might subconsciously *know* the truth. Everyone knew much more than they knew, as it were. For instance, it was pretty certain that the secret of the tranquilomat was locked somewhere down in his unconscious if only he could get at it. Her explanation was logical and worth thinking about.

'You may be right,' he said. 'If so, it's something to go on. But it doesn't stop my reliance on the drug – or the fact that the Man and his helpers are probably telepathic and are at this moment looking for me.'

She nodded. 'Could there be an *antidote* for the drug?'

'Unlikely. Drugs like that don't really need antidotes – they're not like poisons. There must be some way of getting at the people in the fortress – some way of putting a stop to their plans. What about an organized revolution? What has Farlowe tried to do?'

'Nothing much. The people aren't easy to organize. We haven't much to do with one another. Farlowe was probably hoping you could help – think of something he hasn't. Maybe one of those machines you mentioned would work against the fortress people?'

'No, I don't think so. Anyway, the hallucinomats are too big to move from one place to another by hand – let alone from one world to another.'

'And you haven't been able to build a tranquilomat yet?'

'No – we have a lot of experimental machines lying around at the lab – they're fairly small – but it's a question of modifying them – that's what I'm trying to do at the moment. If I could make one that works it would solve part of my problem – it would save my world and perhaps even save yours, if you *are* in a state of conditioning.'

'It sounds reasonable.' She dropped her eyes and looked at her drink. She held the glass balanced on her knees which were pressed closely together, nearly touching him. 'But,' she said, 'they're going to catch you sooner or later. They're very powerful. They're sure to catch you. Then they'll make you agree to their idea.'

'Why are you so certain?'

'I know them.'

He let that go. She said: 'Another drink?' and got up.

'Yes please.' He got up, too, and extended his glass, then went closer to her. She put bottle and glass on the table and looked into his face. There was compassion, mystery, tenderness in her large, dark eyes. He smelled her perfume warm, pleasant. He put his arms around her and kissed her. 'My room,' she said. They went upstairs.

Later that night, feeling strangely revitalized, he left the bed and the sleeping Martha and went and stood beside the window overlooking the silent park. He felt cold and he picked up his shirt and trousers, put them on. He sighed. He felt his mind clear and his body relax. He must work out a way of traveling from this world to his own at will – that might put a stop to the plans of the Man Without A Navel.

He turned guiltily as he heard the door open. Sally was standing there. She wore a long, white, flowing nightdress.

'Lee! I came to tell mummy – what are you doing in

here?' Her eyes were horrified, accusing him. Martha sat up suddenly.

'Sally – what's the matter!'

Lee stepped forward. 'Listen, Sally. Don't —'

Sally shrugged, but tears had come to her eyes. 'I thought you wanted *me*! Now I know – I shouldn't have brought you here. Farlowe said —'

'What did Farlowe say?'

'He said you'd want to marry me!'

'But that's ridiculous. How could he say that? I'm a stranger here. You were to hide me from the fortress people, that's all.'

But she had only picked up one word. 'Ridiculous. Yes, I suppose it is, when my own mother . . .'

'Sally – you'd better go to bed. We'll discuss it in the morning,' said Martha softly. 'What was it you came in about?'

Sally laughed theatrically. 'It doesn't matter now.' She slammed the door.

Seward looked at Martha. 'I'm sorry, Martha.'

'It wasn't your fault – or mine. Sally's romantic and young.'

'And jealous.' Seward sat down on the bed. The feeling of comfort, of companionship, of bringing some order out of chaos – it had all faded. 'Look, Martha, I can't stay here.'

'You're running away?'

'If you like – but – well – the two of you – I'm in the middle.'

'I guessed that. No, you'd better stay. We'll work something out.'

'Okay.' He got up, sighing heavily. 'I think I'll go for a walk in the park – it may help me to think. I'd just reached the stage where I was getting somewhere. Thanks for that anyway, Martha.'

She smiled. 'Don't worry, Lee. I'll have everything running smoothly again by tomorrow.'

He didn't doubt it. She was a remarkable woman.

He put on his socks and shoes, opened the door and went out on to the landing. Moonlight entered through a tall, slender window at the end. He went down the two flights of stairs and out of the front door. He turned into the lane and entered the arbor. In the cool of the night, he once again was able to begin some constructive thinking.

While he was on this world, he would not waste his time, he would keep trying to discover the necessary modifications to make the tranquilomats workable.

He wandered through the arbor, keeping any thoughts of the two women out of his mind. He turned into another section of the arbor he hadn't noticed before. The turnings became numerous but he was scarcely aware of them. It was probably some sort of child's maze.

He paused as he came to a bench. He sat down and folded his arms in front of him, concentrating on his problem.

Much later he heard a sound to his right and looked up.

A man he didn't know was standing there, grinning at him.

Seward noticed at once that the man had overlong canines, that he smelt of damp earth and decay. He wore a black, polo-neck pullover and black, stained trousers. His face was waxen and very pale.

'I've been looking for you for ages, Professor Seward,' said the Vampire.

CHAPTER FIVE

SEWARD GOT up and faced the horrible creature. The Vampire continued to smile. He didn't move. Seward felt revulsion.

'It's been a long journey,' said the Vampire in a sibilant voice like the sound of a frigid wind blowing through dead boughs. 'I had intended to visit you at the fortress, but when I got to your room you had left. I was disappointed.'

'Doubtless,' said Seward. 'Well, you've had a wasted journey. I'm not going back there until I'm ready.'

'That doesn't interest me.'

'What does?' Seward tried to stop himself from trembling.

The Vampire put his hands into his pockets. 'Only you.'

'Get away from here. You're outnumbered – I have friends.' But he knew that his tone was completely unconvincing.

The Vampire hissed his amusement. 'They can't do much, Seward.'

'What are you – some sort of android made to frighten people?'

'No.' The Vampire took a pace forward.

Suddenly he stopped as a voice came faintly from somewhere in the maze.

'Lee! Lee! Where are you?'

It was Sally's voice.

'Stay away, Sally!' Lee called.

'But I was going to warn you. I saw the Vampire from the window. He's somewhere in the park.'

'I know. Go home!'

'I'm sorry about the scene, Lee. I wanted to apologize. It was childish.'

'It doesn't matter.' He looked at the Vampire. He was standing in a relaxed position, hands in pockets, smiling. 'Go home, Sally.'

'She won't, you know,' whispered the Vampire.

Her voice was closer. 'Lee, I must talk to you.'

He screamed: 'Sally – the Vampire's here. Go home. Warn your mother, not me. Get some help if you can – but go home!'

Now he saw her enter the part of the maze he was in. She gasped as she saw them. He was between her and the Vampire.

'Sally – do what I told you.'

But the Vampire's cold eyes widened and he took one hand out of his pocket and crooked a finger. 'Come here, Sally.'

She began to walk forward.

He turned to the Vampire. 'What do you want?'

'Only a little blood – yours, perhaps – or the young lady's.'

'Damn you. Get away. Go back, Sally.' She didn't seem to hear him.

He daren't touch the cold body, the earth-damp clothes. He stepped directly between the girl and the Vampire.

He felt sick, but he reached out his hands and shoved at the creature's body. Flesh yielded, but bone did not. The Vampire held his ground, smiling, staring beyond Seward at the girl.

Seward shoved again and suddenly the creature's arms clamped around him and the grinning, fanged face darted towards his. The thing's breath disgusted him. He struggled, but could not break the Vampire's grasp.

A cold mouth touched his neck. He yelled and kicked. He felt a tiny pricking against his throat. Sally screamed. He heard her turn and run and felt a fraction of relief.

He punched with both fists as hard as he could into the creature's solar plexus. It worked. The Vampire groaned and let go. Seward was disgusted to see that his fangs dripped with blood.

His blood.

Now rage helped him. He chopped at the Vampire's throat. It gasped, tottered, and fell in a sprawl of loose limbs to the ground.

Panting, Seward kicked it in the head. It didn't move.

He bent down and rolled the Vampire over. As far as he could tell it was dead. He tried to remember what he'd read about legendary vampires. Not much. Something about a stake through its heart. Well, that was out.

But the thought that struck him most was that he had fought one of the fortress people – and had won. It was possible to beat them!

He walked purposefully through the maze. It wasn't as tortuous as he'd supposed. Soon he emerged at the arbor entrance near the house. He saw Sally and Martha running toward him. Behind them, another figure lumbered. Farlowe. He had got here fast.

'Seward,' he shouted. 'They said the Vampire had got you!'

'I got him,' said Seward as they came up and stopped.

'What?'

'I beat him.'

'But – that's impossible.'

Seward shrugged. He felt elated. 'Evidently, it's possible,' he said. 'I knocked him out. He seems to be dead – but I suppose you never know with vampires.'

Farlowe was astonished. 'I believe you,' he said, 'but it's fantastic. How did you do it?'

'I got frightened and then angry,' said Seward simply. 'Maybe you've been overawed by these people too long.'

'It seems like it,' Farlowe admitted. 'Let's go and have a look at him. Sally and Martha had better stay behind.'

Seward led him back through the maze. The Vampire was still where he'd fallen. Farlowe touched the corpse with his foot.

'That's the Vampire all right.' He grinned. 'I knew we had a winner in you, son. What are you going to do now?'

'I'm going straight back to the fortress and get this worked out once and for all. Martha gave me an idea yesterday evening and she may well be right. I'm going to try and find out anyway.'

'Better not be overconfident, son.'

'Better than being overcautious.'

'Maybe,' Farlowe agreed doubtfully. 'What's this idea Martha gave you?'

'It's really her idea, complete. Let her explain. She's an intelligent woman – and she's bothered to think about this problem from scratch. I'd advise you to do the same.'

'I'll hear what it is, first. Let's deal with the Vampire and then get back to the house.'

'I'll leave the Vampire to you. I want to use your car.'

'Why?'

'To go back to the fortress.'

'Don't be a fool. Wait until we've got some help.'

'I can't wait that long, Farlowe. I've got other work to do back on my own world.'

'Okay,' Farlowe shrugged.

Farlowe faded.

The maze began to fade.

Explosions in the brain.

Vertigo.

Sickness.

His head ached and he could not breathe. He yelled, but he had no voice. Multicolored explosions in front of his eyes. He was whirling round and round, spinning rapidly. Then he felt a new surface dragging at his feet. He closed his eyes and stumbled against something. He fell on to something soft.

It was his camp bed. He was back in his laboratory.

Seward wasted no time wondering what had happened. He knew more or less. Possibly his encounter with the Vampire had sent him back – the exertion or – of course – the creature had drawn some of his blood. Maybe that was it. He felt the pricking sensation, still. He went to the mirror near the wash-stand. He could just see the little marks in his neck. Further proof that wherever that world was it was as real as the one he was in now.

He went to the table and picked up his notes, then walked into the other room. In one section was a long bench. On it, in various stages of dismantling, were the machines that he had been working on, the tranquilomats that somehow just didn't work. He picked up one of the smallest and checked its batteries, its lenses and its sonic agitator. The idea with this one was to use a combination of light and sound to agitate certain dormant cells in the brain. Long since, psychophysicists had realized that mental abnormality had a chemical as well as a mental cause. Just as a patient with a psychosomatic illness produced all the biological symptoms of whatever disease he thought he had, so did chemistry play a part in brain disorders. Whether the change in the brain cells came first or afterward they weren't sure. But the fact was that the cells could be agitated and the mind, by a mixture of hypnosis and conditioning, could be made to work normally. But it was a long step from knowing this and being able to use the information in the construction of tranquilomats.

Seward began to work on the machine. He felt he was on the right track, at least.

But how long could he keep going before his need for the drug destroyed his will?

He kept going some five hours before his withdrawal symptoms got the better of him.

He staggered toward one of the drug-drawers and fumbled out an ampoule of M-A 19. He staggered into his bedroom and reached for the needle on the table.

He filled the syringe. He filled his veins. He filled his brain with a series of explosions which blew him clean out of his own world into the other.

Fire flew up his spine. Ignited back-brain, ignited mid-brain, ignited fore-brain. Ignited all centers.

EXPLOSION ALL CENTERS.

This time the transition was brief. He was standing in the part of the maze where he'd been when he'd left. The Vampire's corpse was gone. Farlowe had gone, also. He experienced a feeling of acute frustration that he couldn't continue with his work on KLTM-8 – the tranquilomat he'd been modifying when his craving for the M-A 19 took over.

But there was something to do here, too.

He left the maze and walked toward the house. It was dawn and very cold. Farlowe's car was parked there. He noticed the licence number. It seemed different. It now said YOU 009. Maybe he'd mistaken the last digit for a zero last time he'd looked.

The door was ajar. Farlowe and Martha were standing in the hall.

They looked surprised when he walked in.

'I thought the Vampire was peculiar, son,' said Farlowe. 'But yours was the best vanishing act I've ever seen.'

'Martha will explain that, too,' Seward said, not looking at her. 'Has she told you her theory?'

'Yes, it sounds feasible.' He spoke slowly, looking at the floor. He looked up. 'We got rid of the Vampire. Burned him up. He burns well.'

'That's one out of the way, at least,' said Seward. 'How many others are there at the fortress?'

Farlowe shook his head. 'Not sure. How many did you see?'

'The Man Without A Navel, a character called Brother Sebastian who wears a cowl and probably isn't human either, two pleasant gentlemen called Mr. Morl and Mr. Hand – and a man in fancy dress whose name I don't know.'

'There are one or two more,' Farlowe said. 'But it's not their numbers we've got to worry about – it's their power!'

'I think maybe it's overrated,' Steward said.

'You may be right, son.'

'I'm going to find out.'

'You still want my car?'

'Yes. If you want to follow up behind with whatever help you can gather, do that.'

'I will.' Farlowe glanced at Martha. 'What do you think, Martha?'

'I think he may succeed,' she said. 'Good luck, Lee.' She smiled at him in a way that made him want to stay.

'Right,' said Seward. 'I'm going. Hope to see you there.'

'I may be wrong, Lee,' she said warningly. 'It was only an idea.'

'It's the best one I've heard. Goodbye.'

He went out of the house and climbed into the car.

CHAPTER SIX

THE ROAD was white, the sky was blue, the car was red and the countryside was green. Yet there was less clarity about the scenery than Seward remembered. Perhaps it was because he no longer had the relaxing company of Farlowe, because his mind was working furiously and his emotions at full blast.

Whoever had designed the set-up on this world had done it well, but had missed certain details. Seward realized that one of the 'alien' aspects of the world was that everything was just a little too new. Even Farlowe's car looked as if it had just been driven off the production line.

By the early afternoon he was beginning to feel tired and some of his original impetus had flagged. He decided to move in to the side of the road and rest for a short time, stretch his legs. He stopped the car and got out.

He walked over to the other side of the road. It was on a hillside and he could look down over a wide, shallow valley. A river gleamed in the distance, there were cottages and livestock in the fields. He couldn't see the horizon. Far away he saw a great bank of reddish-looking clouds that seemed to swirl and seethe like a restless ocean. For all the *signs* of habitation, the countryside had taken on a desolate quality as if it had been abandoned. He could not believe that there were people living in the cottages and tending the livestock. The whole thing looked like the set for a film. Or a play – a complicated play devised by the Man Without A Navel and his friends – a play in which the fate of a world – possibly two worlds – was at stake.

How soon would the play resolve itself? he wondered, as he turned back toward the car.

A woman was standing by the car. She must have come down the hill while he was looking at the valley. She had long, jet black hair and big, dark eyes. Her skin was tanned dark gold. She had full, extraordinary sensuous lips. She wore a well-tailored red suit, a black blouse, black shoes and black handbag. She looked rather sheepish. She raised her head to look at him and as she did so a lock of her black hair fell over her eyes. She brushed it back.

'Hello,' she said. 'Am I lucky!'

'Are you?'

'I hope so. I didn't expect to find a car on the road. You haven't broken down, have you?' She asked this last question anxiously.

'No,' he said. 'I stopped for a rest. How did you get here?'

She pointed up the hill. 'There's a little track up there – a cattle-track, I suppose. My car skidded and went into a tree. It's a wreck.'

'I'll have a look at it for you.'

She shook her head. 'There's no point – it's a write-off. Can you give me a lift?'

'Where are you going?' he said unwillingly.

'Well, it's about sixty miles that way,' she pointed in the direction he was going. 'A small town.'

It wouldn't take long to drive sixty miles on a road as clear as this with no apparent speed-limit. He scratched his head doubtfully. The woman was a diversion he hadn't expected and, in a way, resented. But she was very attractive. He couldn't refuse her. He hadn't seen any cart-tracks leading off the road. This, as far as he knew, was the only one, but it was possible he hadn't noticed since he didn't know this world. Also, he decided, the woman evidently wasn't involved in the struggle between the fortress people and Farlowe's friends. She was probably just one of the conditioned, living out her life completely unaware of where she was and why. He might be able to get some information out of her.

'Get in,' he said.

'Oh, thanks.' She got in, seeming rather deliberately to show him a lot of leg. He opened his door and slid under the wheel. She sat uncomfortably close to him. He started the engine and moved the car out on to the road again.

'I'm a stranger here,' he began conversationally. 'What about you?'

'Not me – I've lived hereabouts all my life. Where do you come from – stranger?'

He smiled. 'A long way away.'

'Are they all as good looking as you?' It was trite, but it worked. He felt flattered.

'Not any more,' he said. That was true. Maniacs never looked very good. But this wasn't the way he wanted the conversation to go, however nice the direction. He said: 'You're not very heavily populated around here. I haven't seen another car, or another person for that matter, since I set off this morning.'

'It does get boring,' she said. She smiled at him. That and her full body, her musky scent and her closeness, made him breathe more heavily than he would have liked. One thing about this world – the women were considerably less inhibited than on his own. It was a difference in population, perhaps. In an overcrowded world your social behavior must be more rigid, out of necessity.

He kept his hands firmly on the wheel and his eyes on the road, convinced that if he didn't he'd lose control of himself and the car. The result might be a sort of *femme* fatality. His attraction toward Sally and Martha had not been wholly sexual. Yet he had never felt such purely animal attraction as this woman radiated. Maybe, he decided, she didn't know it. He glanced at her. There again, maybe she did.

It said a lot for the woman if she could take his mind so completely off his various problems.

'My name's Magdalen,' she smiled. 'A bit of a mouthful. What's yours?'

It was a relief to find someone here who didn't already know his name. He rejected the unliked Lee and said: 'Bill – Bill Ward.'

'Short and sweet,' she said. 'Not like mine.'

He grunted vaguely, consciously fighting the emotions rising in him. There was a word for them. A simple word – short and sweet – lust. He rather liked it. He'd been somewhat repressed on his home world and had kept a tight censorship on his feelings. Here it was obviously different.

A little later, he gave in. He stopped the car and kissed her. He was surprised at the ease with which he did it. He forgot about the tranquilomats, about the M-A 19, about the fortress. He forgot about everything except her, and that was maybe why he did what he did.

It was as if he was drawn into yet another world – a private world where only he and she had any existence. An enclosed world consisting only of their desire and their need to satisfy it.

Afterward he felt gloomy, regretful and guilty. He started the car savagely. He knew he shouldn't blame her, but he did. He'd wasted time. Minutes were valuable, even seconds. He'd wasted hours.

Beside him she took a headscarf from her bag and tied it over her hair. 'You're in a hurry.'

He pressed the accelerator as far down as he could.

'What's the problem?' she shouted as the engine thudded noisily.

'I've wasted too much time already. I'll drop you off wherever it is you want.'

'Oh, fine. Just one of those things, eh?'

'I suppose so. It was my fault, I shouldn't have picked you up in the first place.'

She laughed. It wasn't a nice laugh. It was a mocking laugh and it seemed to punch him in the stomach.

'Okay,' he said, 'okay.'

He switched on the headlamps as dusk became night. There was no milometer on the dashboard so he didn't know how far they'd traveled, but he was sure it was more than sixty miles.

'Where is this town?' he said.

'Not much further.' Her voice softened. 'I'm sorry, Lee.

But what *is* the matter?'

Something was wrong. He couldn't place it. He put it down to his own anger.

'You may not know it,' he said, 'but I suspect that nearly all the people living here are being deceived. Do you know the fortress?'

'You mean that big building on the rock wastes?'

'That's it. Well, there's a group of people there who are duping you and the rest in some way. They want to destroy practically the whole of the human race by a particularly nasty method – and they want me to do it for them.'

'What's that?'

Briefly, he explained.

Again she laughed. 'By the sound of it, you're a fool to fight this Man Without A Navel and his friends. You ought to throw in your lot with them. You could be top man.'

'Aren't you angry?' he said in surprise. 'Don't you believe me?'

'Certainly. I just don't share your attitude. I don't understand your turning down a chance when it's offered. I'd take it. As I said, you could be top man.'

'I've already been top man,' he said, 'in a manner of speaking. On my own world. I don't want that kind of responsibility. All I want to do is save something from the mess I've made of civilization.'

'You're a fool, Lee.'

That was it. She shouldn't have known him as Lee but as Bill, the name he'd introduced himself by. He stopped the car suddenly and looked at her suspiciously. The truth was dawning on him and it made him feel sick at himself that he could have fallen for her trap.

'You're working for him, aren't you. The Man?'

'You seem to be exhibiting all the symptoms of persecution mania, Seward. You need a good psychiatrist.' She spoke coolly and reached into her handbag. 'I don't feel safe with you.'

'It's mutual,' he said. 'Get out of the car.'

'No,' she said quietly. 'I think we'll go all the way to the fortress together.' She put both hands into her bag. They came out with two things. One was a half bottle of brandy.

The other was a gun.

'Evidently my delaying tactics weren't effective enough,' she mocked. 'I thought they might not be, so I brought these. Get out yourself, Seward.'

'You're going to kill me?'

'Maybe.'

'But that isn't what The Man wants, is it?'

She shrugged, waving the gun.

Trembling with anger at his own gullibility and impotence, he got out. He couldn't think clearly.

She got out, too, keeping him covered. 'You're a clever man, Seward. You've worked out a lot.'

'There are others here who know what I know.'

'What do they know?'

'They know about the set-up – about the conditioning.'

She came round the car towards him, shaking her head. Still keeping him covered, she put the brandy bottle down on the seat.

He went for the gun.

He acted instinctively, in the knowledge that this was his only chance. He heard the gun go off, but he was forcing her wrist back. He slammed it down on the side of the car. She yelled and dropped it. Then he did what he had never thought he could do. He hit her, a short, sharp jab under the chin. She crumpled.

He stood over her, trembling. Then he took her headscarf and tied her limp hands behind her. He dragged her up and dumped her in the back of the car. He leant down and found the gun. He put it in his pocket.

Then he got into the driving seat, still trembling. He felt something hard under him. It was the brandy bottle. It was what he needed. He unscrewed the cap and took a long drink.

His brain began to explode even as he reached for the ignition.

It seemed to crackle and flare like burning timber. He grabbed the door handle. Maybe if he walked around . . .

He felt his knees buckle as his feet touched the ground. He strained to keep himself upright. He forced himself to move round the car. When he reached the bonnet, the headlamps glared at him, blinded him.

They began to blink rapidly into his eyes. He tried to raise his hands and cover his eyes. He fell sideways, the lights still blinking. He felt nausea sweep up and through him. He saw the car's licence plate in front of him.

YOU 099

YOU 100

YOU 101

He put out a hand to touch the plate. It seemed normal. Yet the digits were clocking up like numbers on an adding machine.

Again his brain exploded. A slow, leisurely explosion that subsided and brought a delicious feeling of well-being.

Green clouds like boiled jade, scent of chrysanthemums. Swaying lilies. Bright lines of black and white in front of his eyes. He shut them and opened them again. He was looking up at the blind in his bedroom.

As soon as he realized he was back, Seward jumped off the bed and made for the bench where he'd left the half-finished tranquilomat. He remembered something, felt for the gun he'd taken off the girl. It wasn't there.

But he felt the taste of the brandy in his mouth. Maybe it was as simple as that, he thought. Maybe all he needed to get back was alcohol.

There was sure to be some alcohol in the lab. He searched through cupboards and drawers until he found some in a jar. He filled a vial and corked it. He took off his shirt and taped the vial under his armpit – that way he might be able to transport it from his world to the other one.

Then he got down to work.

Lenses were re-assembled, checked. New filters went in and old ones came out. He adjusted the resonators and amplifiers. He was recharging the battery which powered the transistorized circuits, when he sensed the mob outside. He left the little machine on the bench and went to the control board. He flicked three switches down and then, on impulse, flicked them off again. He went back to the bench and unplugged the charger. He took the machine to the window. He drew the blind up.

It was a smaller mob than usual. Evidently some of them had learned their lesson and were now avoiding the laboratory.

Far away, behind them, the sun glinted on a calm sea. He opened the window.

There was one good way of testing his tranquilomat. He rested it on the sill and switched it to ATTRACT. That was the first necessary stage, to hold the mob's attention. A faint, pleasant humming began to come from the machine. Seward knew that specially shaped and colored lenses were whirling at the front. The mob looked up towards it, but only those in the center of the group were held. The others dived away, hiding their eyes.

Seward felt his body tightening, growing cold. Part of him began to scream for the M-A 19. He clung to the machine's carrying handles. He turned a dial from Zero to 50. There were 100 units marked on the indicator. The machine was now sending at half-strength. Seward consoled himself that if anything went wrong he could not do any more harm to their ruined minds. It wasn't much of a consolation.

He quickly saw that the combined simulated brainwaves, sonic vibrations and light patterns were having some effect on their minds. But what was the effect going to be? They were certainly responding. Their bodies were relaxing, their faces were no longer twisted with insanity. But was the tranquilomat actually doing any constructive good – what it had been designed to do? He upped the output to 75 degrees.

His hand began to tremble. His mouth and throat were

tight and dry. He couldn't keep going. He stepped back. His stomach ached. His bones ached. His eyes felt puffy. He began to move towards the machine again. But he couldn't make it. He moved toward the half-full ampoule of M-A 19 on the table. He filled the blunt hypodermic. He found a vein. He was weeping as the explosion hit his brain.

CHAPTER SEVEN

THIS TIME it was different. He saw an army of machines advancing towards him. An army of malevolent hallucinomats. He tried to run, but a thousand electrodes were clamped to his body and he could not move. From nowhere, needles entered his veins. Voices shouted SEWARD! SEWARD! SEWARD! The hallucinomats advanced, shrilling, blinking, buzzing – *laughing*. The machines were laughing at him.

SEWARD!

Now he saw Farlowe's car's registration plate.

YOU 110

YOU 111

YOU 119

SEWARD!

YOU!

SEWARD!

His brain was being squeezed. It was contracting, contracting. The voices became distant, the machines began to recede. When they had vanished he saw he was standing in a circular room in the centre of which was a low dais. On the dais was a chair. In the chair was the Man Without A Navel. He smiled at Seward.

'Welcome back, old boy,' he said.

Brother Sebastian and the woman, Magdalen, stood close to the dais. Magdalen's smile was cool and merciless, seeming to anticipate some new torture that the Man and Brother Sebastian had devised.

But Seward was jubilant. He was sure his little tranquilomat had got results.

'I think I've done it,' he said quietly. 'I think I've built a workable tranquilomat – and, in a way it's thanks to you. I had to speed my work up to beat you – and I did it!'

They seemed unimpressed.

'Congratulations, Seward,' smiled the Man Without A Navel. 'But this doesn't alter the situation, you know. Just because you *have* an antidote doesn't mean we have to use it.'

Seward reached inside his shirt and felt for the vial taped under his arm. It had gone. Some of his confidence went with the discovery.

Magdalen smiled. 'It was kind of you to drink the drugged brandy.'

He put his hands in his jacket pocket.

The gun was back there. He grinned.

'What's he smiling at?' Magdalen said nervously.

'I don't know. It doesn't matter. Brother Sebastian, I believe you have finished work on your version of Seward's hypomat?'

'I have,' said the sighing, cold voice.

'Let's have it in. It is a pity we didn't have it earlier. It would have saved us time – and Seward all his efforts.'

The curtains behind them parted and Mr. Hand, Mr. Morl and the Laughing Cavalier wheeled in a huge, bizarre machine that seemed to have a casing of highly-polished gold, silver and platinum. They looked like eyes staring at Seward.

Was this a conditioning machine like the ones they'd probably used on the human populace? Seward thought it was likely. If they got him with that, he'd be finished. He pulled the gun out of his pocket. He aimed it at the right-hand lens and pulled the trigger.

The gun roared and kicked in his hand, but no bullet left the muzzle. Instead there came a stream of small brightly coloured globes, something like those used in the attraction device on the tranquilomat. They sped toward the machine, struck it, exploded. The machine buckled and shrilled. It steamed and two discs, like lids, fell across the lenses. The machine rocked backwards and fell over.

The six figures began to converge on him, angrily.

Suddenly, on his left, he saw Farlowe, Martha and Sally step from behind a screen.

'Help me!' he cried to them.

'We can't!' Farlowe yelled. 'Use your initiative, son!'

'Initiative?' he looked down at the gun. The figures were coming closer. The Man Without A Navel smiled slowly. Brother Sebastian tittered. Magdalen gave a low mocking laugh that seemed – strangely – to be a criticism of his sexual prowess. Mr. Morl and Mr. Hand retained their mournful and cheerful expressions respectively. The Laughing Cavalier flung back his head and – laughed. All around them the screens, which had been little more than head-high, were lengthening, widening, stretching up and up.

He glanced back. The screens were growing.

He pulled the trigger of the gun. Again it bucked, again it roared – and from the muzzle came a stream of metallic-gray particles which grew into huge flowers. The flowers burst into flame and formed a wall between him and the six.

He peered around him, looking for Farlowe and the others. He couldn't find them. He heard Farlowe shout 'Good luck, son!' He heard Martha and Sally crying goodbye. 'Don't go!' he yelled.

Then he realized he was alone. And the six were beginning to advance again – malevolent, vengeful.

Around him the screens, covered in weird designs that curled and swirled, ever-changing, were beginning to topple inwards. In a moment he would be crushed.

Again he heard his name being called. SEWARD! SEWARD!

Was it Martha's voice? He thought so.

'I'm coming,' he shouted, and pulled the trigger again.

The Man Without A Navel, Magdalen, Brother Sebastian, the Laughing Cavalier, Mr. Hand and Mr. Morl – all screamed in unison and began to back away from him as the gun's muzzle spouted a stream of white fluid which floated into the air.

Still the screens were falling, slowly, slowly.

The white fluid formed a net of millions of delicate strands. It drifted over the heads of the six. It began to descend. They looked up and screamed again.

'Don't, Seward,' begged the Man Without A Navel. 'Don't, old man – I'll make it worth your while.'

Seward watched as the net engulfed them. They struggled and cried and begged.

It did not surprise him much when they began to shrink.

No! *They* weren't shrinking – he was growing. He was growing over the toppling screens. He saw them fold inwards. He looked down and the screens were like cards folding neatly over the six little figures struggling in the white net. Then, as the screens folded down, the figures were no longer in sight. It got lighter. The screens rolled themselves into a ball.

The ball began to take on a new shape.

It changed colour. And then, there it was – a perfectly formed human skull.

Slowly, horrifyingly, the skull began to gather flesh and blood and muscles to itself. The stuff flowed over it. Features began to appear. Soon, in a state of frantic terror, Seward recognized the face.

It was his own.

His own face, its eyes wide, its lips parted. A tired, stunned, horrified face.

He was back in the laboratory. And he was staring into a mirror.

He stumbled away from the mirror. He saw he wasn't holding a gun in his hand but a hypodermic needle. He looked round the room.

The tranquilomat was still on the window-sill. He went to the window. There, quietly talking among the ruins below, was a group of sane men and women. They were still in rags, still gaunt. But they were sane. That was evident. They were saner than they had ever been before.

He called down to them, but they didn't hear him.

Time for that later, he thought. He sat on the bed, feeling dazed and relieved. He dropped the needle to the floor, certain he wouldn't need to use it again.

It was incredible, but he thought he knew where he had been. The final image of his face in the mirror had given him the last clue.

He had been inside his own mind. The M-A 19 was merely a hallucinogenic after all. A powerful one, evidently, if it could give him the illusion of rope-marks on his wrists, bites on his neck and the rest.

He had escaped into a dream world.

Then he wondered – but why? What good had it done?

He got up and went toward the mirror again.

Then he heard the voice. Martha's voice.

SEWARD! SEWARD! Seward, listen to me!

No, he thought desperately. No, it can't be starting again. There's no need for it.

He ran into the laboratory, closing the door behind him, locking it. He stood there, trembling, waiting for the withdrawal symptoms. They didn't come.

Instead he saw the walls of the laboratory, the silent computers and meters and dials, begin to blurr. A light flashed on above his head. The dead bank of instruments suddenly came alive. He sat down in a big chrome padded chair which had originally been used for the treating of test-subjects.

His gaze was caught by a whirling stroboscope that had appeared from nowhere. Coloured images began to form in front of his eyes. He struggled to get up but he couldn't.

YOU 121

YOU 122

YOU 123

Then the first letter changed to a V.

VOU 127

SEWARD!

His eyelids fell heavily over his eyes.

'Professor Seward.' It was Martha's voice. It spoke to someone else. 'We may be lucky, Tom. Turn down the volume.'

He opened his eyes.

'Martha.'

The woman smiled. She was dressed in a white coat and was leaning over the chair. She looked very tired. 'I'm not – Martha – Professor Seward. I'm Doctor Kalin. Remember?'

'Doctor Kalin, of course.'

His body felt weaker than it had ever felt before. He leaned back in the big chair and sighed. Now he was remembering.

It had been his decision to make the experiment. It had seemed to be the only way of speeding up work on the development of the tranquilomats. He knew that the secret of a workable machine was imbedded in the deepest level of his unconscious mind. But, however much he tried – hypnosis, symbol-association, word-association – he couldn't get at it.

There was only one way he could think of – a dangerous experiment for him – an experiment which might not work at all. He would be given a deep-conditioning, made to believe that he had brought disaster to the world and must remedy it by devising a tranquilomat. Things were pretty critical in the world outside, but they weren't as bad as they had conditioned him to believe. Work on the tranquilomats *was* falling behind – but there had been no widespread disaster, *yet*. It was bound to come unless they could devise some means of mass-cure for the thousands of neurotics and victims of insanity. An antidote for the results of mass-tension.

So, simply, they conditioned him to think his efforts had destroyed civilization. He must devise a working tranquilomat. They had turned the problem from an intellectual one into a personal one.

The conditioning had apparently worked.

He looked around the laboratory at his assistants. They were all alive, healthy, a bit tired, a bit strained, but they looked relieved.

'How long have I been under?' he asked.

'About fourteen hours. That's twelve hours since the experiment went wrong.'

'Went wrong?'

'Why, yes,' said Doctor Kalin in surprise. 'Nothing was happening. We tried to bring you round – we tried every darned machine and drug in the place – nothing worked. We expected catatonia. At least we've managed to save you. We'll just have to go on using the ordinary methods of research, I suppose.' Her voice was tired, disappointed.

Seward frowned. But he *had* got the results. He knew exactly how to construct a working tranquilomat. He thought back.

'Of course,' he said. 'I was only conditioned to believe that the world was in ruins and I had done it. There was nothing about – about – the *other* world.

'What other world?' Macpherson, his Chief Assistant, asked the question.

Seward told them. He told them about the Man Without A Navel, the fortress, the corridors, the tortures, the landscapes seen from Farlowe's car, the park, the maze, the Vampire, Magdalen . . . He told them how, in what he now called Condition A, he had believed himself hooked on a drug called M-A 19.

'But we don't have a drug called M-A 19,' said Doctor Kalin.

'I know that now. But I didn't know then and it didn't matter. I would have found something to have made the journey into – the other world – a world existing only in my skull. Call it Condition B, if you like – or Condition X, maybe. The unknown. I found a fairly logical means of making myself *believe* I was entering another world. That was M-A 19. By inventing symbolic characters who were trying to stop me, I made myself work harder. Unconsciously I knew that Condition A was going wrong – so I escaped into Condition B in order to put right the damage. By acting out the drama I was able to clear my mind of its confusion. I had, as I suspected, the secret of the tranquilomat somewhere down there all the time. Condition A failed to release that secret – Condition B succeeded. I can build you a workable tranquilomat, don't worry.'

'Well,' Macpherson grinned. 'I've been told to use my imagination in the past – but you *really* used yours!'

'That was the idea, wasn't it? We'd decided it was no good just using drugs to keep us going. We decided to use our drugs and hallucinomats directly, to condition me to believe that what we feared will happen, *had* happened.'

'I'm glad we didn't manage to bring you back to normality, in that case,' Doctor Kalin smiled. 'You've had a series of classic – if more complicated than usual – nightmares. The Man Without A Navel, as you call him, and his "allies" symbolized the elements in you that were holding you back from the truth – diverting you. By "defeating" the Man, you defeated those elements.'

'It was a hell of a way to get results,' Seward grinned. 'But I got them. It was probably the only way. Now we can produce as many tranquilomats as we need. The problem's over. I've – in all modesty –' he grined, 'saved the world before it needed saving. It's just as well.'

'What about your "helpers," though?' said Doctor Kalin, helping him from the chair. He glanced into her intelligent mature face. He had always liked her.

'Maybe,' he smiled, as he walked towards the bench where the experimental tranquilomats were laid out, 'maybe there was quite a bit of wish-fulfilment mixed up in it as well.'

'It's funny how you didn't realize that it wasn't real, isn't it?' said Macpherson behind him.

'Why is it funny?' he turned to look at Macpherson's long, worn face. 'Who knows what's real, Macpherson. This world? That world? Any other world? I don't feel so adamant about this one, do you?'

'Well . . .' Macpherson said doubtfully, 'I mean, you're a trained psychiatrist as well as everything else. You'd think you'd recognize your own symbolic characters?'

'I suppose it's possible.' Macpherson had missed his point. 'All the same,' he added, 'I wouldn't mind going back there some day. I'd quite enjoy the exploration. And I liked some of the people. Even though they were probably wish-fulfilment figures. Farlowe – father – it's possible.' He glanced up as his eye fell on a meter. It consisted of a series of code-letters and three digits. VOU 128 it said now. There was Farlowe's number-plate. His mind had turned the V into a Y. He'd probably discover plenty of other symbols around, which he'd turned into something else in the other world. He still couldn't think of it as a dream world. It had seemed so real. For him, it was still real.

'What about the woman – Martha?' Doctor Kalin said. 'You called *me* Martha as you were waking up.'

'We'll let that one go for the time being,' he grinned. 'Come on, we've still got a lot of work to do.'

All the Weed in the World

FRITZ LEIBER

WHEN YOU first smoke marijuana (the Professor said) there are all sorts of kicks the old teahounds will try to steer you into to heighten your enjoyment. Some of them are pretty much at the physical level, like getting loaded and eating a cheap cafeteria meal to see how much more intensely good it tastes than your sober imagination of a gourmet's feast, or taking a simple amusement-park roller-coaster ride and discovering space flight. Others call on the imagination a little more. There are several pretty obvious ones involving all the most beautiful girls in the world – or if your fellow weed-heads are intellectual you may be guided into imagined converse with all the great musicians of the past and all the great artists and writers. Liszt may play your inner piano, Paganini your violin, Poe may tread behind you on a midnight walk reciting his poetry. Some of these kicks can be very simple. My teacher put his hand lightly on my head as I sipped that first drag and he told me to close my eyes and then he said softly, 'You're just a little weed growing in the desert and the wind is blowing through you.' Of course he meant the marijuana weed – weed itself.

If you're young and previously unacquainted with drugs and with intense creative activity (the Professor continued briskly), you may take this imaginative bait and have a few memorable bangs before the first flush fades away forever and you quit all drugs if you've got sense. It'll be like you wrote a beautiful poem without ever writing it. If you're older and have done some heavy drinking and so on, you probably won't respond at all and you'll tell your well-meaning mentors that weed is much overrated.

But there's one kick they'll try to give you that will almost certainly work for you at least once, whether you're a fresh kid or a dull codger. It's one of the biggest and best and simplest kicks there is, and it involves another 'all.' And it's a good kick. (The bad kicks, like knowing that all the cops in the world are just outside that green door, will come whether you're steered into them or not.) This kick is about all the weed in the world – but before I tell it I've got to tell you about the old doctor.

This ancient six-foot-three-inch wreck – a rain-streaked, fire-blackened ruin of a man with a few bats already flitting through his warped and paintless belfry and a few worms already gnawing at his toes inside his size-fifteen shoes with their little black hangnails of peeling leather – this walking catastrophe had got his M.D. from a homeopathic college back at the turn of the century. He'd occupied the same office for forty years – already the building was changing over from offices to slum apartments – and he was to go on occupying it until he died and they tore the building down. And he was a confirmed miser – he had a box of string (each piece coiled like a rattlesnake) and a box of dead rubber bands (maybe the strings had bit 'em) and barrels of pharmaceutical samples going back to 1900, and already the newspapers had started to pile up ominously in the corners. Even by middle-class standards his office was a dark and cluttered hole with sooty green walls, but it was good enough for his dollar patients and for me, who paid him five to write me morphine prescriptions. In fact to me his office was a dim dark restful shrine that soothed my jitters as if the black dust of the walls were loaded with cocaine. Eventually we got to know each other well, and by bits and pieces he told me his story.

In his youth this old stricken eagle, this thunder-blasted tree, had had a great dream to which he had dedicated his whole life. It had come to him while he was interning at a primitive mental hospital – a vision of healing the sick minds of mankind with narcotic drugs alone. Remember this was back in the days when the opiates were on the open market, when even Sigmund Freud briefly thought the newly-discovered cocaine was great for everyday use (at least by a young and vigorous psychiatrist), when the best thing you could do for a mental case was to keep him soothed down and quiet. (They still have that last idea, why else lobotomy?)

Today it is hard for us to visualize how lightly people regarded narcotic drugs then (the Professor said wistfully) and how easy they were to purchase. The Harrison Narcotic Act of 1914 wiped them off the legal market faster than Roosevelt banned dealings in gold.

At any rate, the old doctor (young then) had the inspiration that there must be a specific narcotic drug that in massive doses would cure each recognized form of insanity. He even had them provisionally identified – morphine for mania, codeine for hysteria, cocaine for involutional melancholia, heroin for catatonia, laudanum (though it's no single drug) for dementia praecox, and so on. Somehow the old doctor never got on drugs himself, but his theory was worthy of a King Weedhead – actually it is quite a kick just by itself.

There wasn't much he could do then to test his theory – he didn't have the reputation or a private sanitarium – but he could prepare to test it. At that time the most important preparation was to get hold of an adequate supply of the drugs he'd need. Narcotics were still openly purchasable, but they wouldn't be for long. The Shanghai Conference and the Hague Convention were coming up and the Harrison Act was already a little black cloud on the horizon. The old doctor didn't want mankind to miss out on the boon he was readying for it just because soon even he, a licensed physician, wouldn't be able to get hold of the essential drugs in the large quantities he'd need, so for the next few years he sank all his spare cash in narcotics, purchasing them all over the country and trying to make sure that he had an adequate supply of every known drug – because he couldn't be certain yet just which narcotic would prove to be the specific remedy for each form of insanity. Even after the passage of the Harrison Act, he continued in a small way to build up his stock, especially of newly discovered drugs, through the regular medical channels available to him.

A few years later he got a fine opportunity to test his great theory: his wife went crazy, and a little later their two children took off in the same direction. He shot them each full of what he considered was the right drug. His theory didn't work. One by one, he had to ship them off to the asylum.

That was the little tragedy that finished the old doctor as a dreamer (the Professor said softly). That was the lightning bolt that blackened and blasted him, that started the first bats winging through his lonely belfry, that turned him into a miserly automaton. Being an addict, I often wondered what happened to his great stockpile of drugs, but that was one point where the old doctor got cagey with me. He'd never quite say. I suppose I assumed that he'd sold them or used them somehow in the natural course of things – after all, would he be writing morphine prescriptions for me if he could with greater saftey and profit be selling me some? Besides, his great dream had been dead for twenty years or so when we had our little talks.

What I forgot was the degree of his miserliness and the rigidity of his automatism. There were larger and hairier bats in his belfry than I ever guessed.

I soon drifted away from the city and the old doctor (sighed the Professor), partly to take an involuntary cure for my addiction at Lexington. The cure didn't altogether work, but eventually I did make the unusual but not unheard-of transition to alcohol. At any rate, when I got back to the city again I was a wino and (what is almost a tautology) I was broke. I looked up my friend the old doctor and he was dead and they were tearing down the building he'd practiced in for over fifty years.

For the next week or so I camped nights in that half-destroyed building. It was a convenient den and the dead old doctor's dismantled office – still with the same soot-drifted green walls – was a closer approximation to home for me than any other spot in the known world. I remember I dripped a couple of tears the night I dragged myself and my jug up the crazy stairs and came to the familiar doorway – and discovered just in time that they'd knocked the floor out of his place that day. The green wall across from me was still up, though the plaster and laths had started to fall away here and there, but in between was just a pit unevenly floored with rubble two stories down.

That night I camped in the room across the hall, where there was still a floor. It must have been almost dawn when I woke up coughing. The air was full of smoke and the floor was hot and I heard distant sirens. I struggled into the hall and there the heat really hit me.

Light flared through the old doctor's door. Someone (another crazy wino probably) had set fire to what was left of the building. The floor below and the opposite wall were ablaze. And at the very moment I looked in, a big section of flaming lath and green-crusted plaster fell away right across from me, revealing a dark space behind it that had been hidden for decades.

Now pause (the Professor said) and recall that I was going to tell you about a kick involving all the weed in the world. For this kick, you simply imagine that all the weed in the world has been harvested and dried and variously processed and then gathered in one spot close by you – all the reefers, all the joints, all the hemp, all the bhang, kif, takrouri, dagga, charas, mutah, manzoul, maconha, djamba, ganja, esrar, dynamite, tea, pot, stick, gauge, grass, yummy (for those are all names that have been used for marijuana) – and that someone has set fire to this resinous and ecstasy-loaded haystack and that you are sitting at a comfortable distance downwind from it, inhaling the beatific smoke.

Back to the real fire now and to me crouching in the old doctor's doorway and staring across the floorless space at the wall opposite – a wall as far away from me as that of China, as far as my ability to reach it went.

The dark space revealed by the falling lath and plaster was not empty, but neatly lined with shelves, and on the shelves were all manner of boxes and tins and bottles – big bottles with glass stoppers, filled mostly with white powders and crystals. Already one or two of the bottles had burst with the heat and the bold labels were blackening, but I could read enough of them to tell the story – and I'm sure I could have guessed the story without any labels at all.

Even as I watched, a few more bottles exploded and the local flames sprang up more fiercely. Most of the opiates are highly inflammable, you know – people *smoke* opium – they're unsaturated hydrocarbons.

So there I crouched and watched them burn – not fifteen feet away from me but absolutely inaccessible. The white crystaline morphine and heroin and cocaine, great swelling jars of it. The tins of black bubbling opium with the pale blue flames shooting up. Hashish melting and flaming and running like some lava of the Eastern gods. The tall sealed beaker of ruby-red laudanum – *that* really set everything blazing when it burst, for laudanum is opium dissolved in alcohol. The big bottles of melting barbiturate capsules – red seconal, blue Amytal, yellow Nembutal, phenobarbital, tuinal, Veronal. Oily, hot-burning chloral and paraldehyde. Volatile chloroform and the devil-god ether – *there* were explosions for you! And all the endless others that the old doctor had gathered in his crazy quest – pantopon, paregoric, papaverine, novocaine, procaine, thebaine, narcotine, narceine, codeine, Dilaudid, Dicodide, Dionin – all, all burning, burning completely and utterly.

I didn't hear the fire engines arriving or the hoses sizzling into the flames, or the firemen finally clumping up the stairs behind me. I just crouched there witless, staring and sniffing, until I blacked out.

The firemen found me in time, though I sometimes think that was the worst thing that ever happened to me. I woke up in the city hospital, telling my story over and over again to anyone who'd listen. I honestly think I was still higher than a kite on the variegated fumes I'd sniffed.

Of course everyone told me the old building burned down completely, and that was so.

All my big mouth should have got me was trouble (the Professor finished) except no one believed that my story was anything but a wino's vision, an old hophead's dream.

The Roger Bacon Formula

FLETCHER PRATT

I MET THE old man as the result of three beers and an argument. I never even knew his name. He may be one of the greatest scientists alive; he may even not have been human; and in either of these cases, I would hold through him the key to an almost infinite enrichment of the human spirit. On the other hand, he may merely have been one of those people of whom the law takes a justifiably dim view, and in that case, it wouldn't even do for me to be inquiring after him. I work in a bank, and it would be as much as my job is worth.

So all I have is a rather incredible story. All right, I admit I wouldn't believe it myself if somebody else told it. But just listen, will you? You can check if you want to.

It starts in one of those restaurant-bars in Greenwich Village, where they have booths opposite the bar, a radio that goes all the time, and as little light as possible. The gang used to meet there because it was less depressing than getting together in anyone's furnished room and just about as cheap as long as you stuck to beer. It was a good gang, even if most of them were a bunch of lousy Reds – or thought they were in those days. I noticed that with most of them, the closer they got to fifty bucks a week, the farther they got from the party line. That was the dividing line, fifty per; once they hit it, they were all through as Commies.

At the time I'm telling about, it was different, and I was practically the only one who blew a fuse whenever the name of Karl Marx was mentioned. They used to gang up on me, with a lot of scientific terms, and they knew most of the arguments I used, so I was always having to think up new ones. On this night I'm talking about, I'd been doing a little reading, so I let them have it with something about Roger Bacon, the medieval friar, you know, who did so much monkeying around both with philosophy and the physical sciences. 'Go on, look him up some time,' I told them. 'You'll find that every real argument of the Marxian dialectic has been anticipated and answered before it was ever written down. Marx was just ignoramus enough not to know that he was digging up dead rats.'

That let things loose, especially as none of them really knew any more about Roger Bacon than I did, and for that matter, they hadn't read Marx at first hand, either. We all talked loud enough to keep down the noise of the radio and to try to keep down each other, so that after about the third beer, the bartender came around and told us to pipe down a little. I had had my fun by that time, so I tried to change the subject to something safe, like baseball, and when the rest wouldn't, I got up and went home.

Or started for home. I was just going around the corner when this old man sidled up to me. 'Pardon me, sir,' he said apologetically.

The Village is full of panhandlers. I glanced at him for long enough to see that he was very short, had white hair and no hat, and a tear in his coat. I said, 'Sorry, chum, I haven't got any money.'

'I don't want money,' he said. 'It's about – that is, I heard you mention Roger Bacon.'

I looked at him again then. He had a kind of pear-shaped head with a little fluffy crown of hair on the top of it, and a rim of more hair around over the ears, and the longest and thinnest hands I ever saw on a human being. The tendons stood out on the backs of those hands and made it look as though there were no flesh between them at all. I said, 'I'm afraid I'm really not much of a Bacon student.'

He looked so disappointed that I thought he was going to

burst into tears. I tried to comfort him with, 'But I do think the Bacon manuscripts are remarkable productions, whether they are forged or not.'

'Forged?' he said, his voice going up thinly. 'I don't ... Oh, you mean the Parma manuscripts, the ones Newbold tried to translate when he achieved such curiously correct results by the wrong method. But those only describe annular eclipses and plant reproduction. They are the least part of the work. If the world had listened to the full doctrine of Roger Bacon, it would be six centuries further along the path of civilization.'

'Do you think so?' I said. This sounded like the beginning of one of the arguments of the gang.

'I know it! Can you spare a few moments to come up to my place? I have something that will interest any student of Roger Bacon. There are so few.'

If there is one thing the Village has more of than panhandlers, it is nuts, but the night was young and the old bird sounded so wistful that it was hard to turn him down. Besides, even a nut can be interesting. I let him lead me around a couple of corners to Bank Street and up interminable flights of stairs in a rickety building to where he flung open a door on an attic room of surprising size.

Its layout resembled the tower of a medieval alchemist more than anything it could have been designed for. There was a long library table in black wood, stained and scarred, on which stood a genuine alembic, which had been abandoned to distill some pungent liquid over a low flame. All around about the alembic was a furious litter of papers, chemical apparatus and bottled reagents. A cabinet opposite held rolls of something that appeared to be sheepskin; there was a sextant on the cot, a telescope stood by the window. To complete the picture, a huge armillary sphere occupied the corner of the room between the cot and the telescope.

I realized the old duffer was talking in his piping voice: '– the unity of all the sciences, Roger Bacon's greatest contribution to human knowledge. Your modern specialists are only beginning to realize that every experimenter must understand other sciences before he can begin to deal with his own. What would the zoologist do without a knowledge of some chemistry, the chemist without geology, and the geologist without physics? Science is all one. I will show —'

He was at the cabinet, producing one of the sheepskin rolls. It was covered with the crabbed and illegible writing of the Middle Ages, made more illegible still by the wear and tear of centuries.

'A genuine Roger Bacon. You know there are some years following his stay in Paris that have never been accounted for publicly? Ha! Certainly you do not know that he spent them at Citeaux, the headquarters of the order to which he belonged. I have been to Citeaux. I found them restoring the place after the damage caused by the war. Fortunate circumstance that you – that we have wars. The vaults had been damaged by shellfire; it was easy to search among them and gather – these!' He waved one of his skeleton-like hands toward the sheepskin rolls. 'The greatest of Roger Bacon's works.'

'But didn't the French government —?' I asked.

'French government! What does any government that represents only a tiny portion of the world know about something that affects the whole? The French government never heard of the manuscripts. I saw to that.' He chuckled.

'What did you find in them?' I asked.

'Everything. What would you say to an absolutely flat statement of the nebular hypothesis? An exposition of nuclear theory?'

'It must be wonderful. Is that all in there?' I was not quite sure what he was talking about, but I knew enough to know I should be startled.

'All that and more. Didn't I tell you that Bacon made discoveries that the rest of the world has not yet grasped? Here look at this —' He shoved one of the sheepskins into my hand. 'Wait, you do not know how to read the script. I have the same thing written out and translated.' He fumbled among the papers on the laboratory table and handed me one. His own writing was almost as bad as the medieval script, but I managed to make out something like this:

'*De Transpositio mentis*: He that would let hys spirit vade within the launds of fay and fell shall drinke of the drogge mandragoreum till he bee sight out of eye, sowne out of ear, speache out of lips and time out of minde. Lapped in lighte shall he then fare toe many a straunge and horrid earthe beyond the bounds of ocean and what he seeth there shall astounde him much; yet shall he return withouten any hurt.'

'What do you make of it?' said the old man.

'That he was probably a drug addict,' I said, frankly. 'Mandragora is fairly well known – was well known even in the Middle Ages, I presume.'

'You are as bad as the rest,' said the old man. 'I had hoped that a Bacon scholar – look, you're missing all the essentials. You people here never believe in anything but yourselves. Now, look again. He doesn't say "mandragora" but "mandragoreum," and it's not a copyist's error, because it's written in Bacon's own hand. Note also that he titles it "the transposition of the mind." He never imagined, as drug addicts do, that his body was performing strange things. What Roger Bacon is telling us there is that there is a drug which will bring about the dissociation of the mind from the body which seems to occur under hypnotism, but "withouten any hurt." Also he says "lapped in lighte," which is more than a hint of employing the force and speed of light. Modern science has not attained anything like that yet. I told you Bacon was ahead not only of his time, but of ours. Moreover – ' here he gave me a quick glance ' – in another place, I found the formula for compounding his drug mandragoreum, and I can assure you that it is nothing like mandragora. I have even used it myself; it produces a certain ionization among the cells of the inner brain by action on the pineal – but you probably don't understand; you are willing to remain earthbound.'

I looked at him, trying to figure out what he was driving at. Was he suggesting that I try out this mandragoreum of his? And why me? Surely, if there were anything in it —

'You doubt me? I grant it sounds incredible. Your scientists, as they call themselves, would laugh. But here, try it for yourself. It is the authentic mandragoreum of Bacon.' He seized the flask into which the alembic had discharged its contents and thrust it into my hand.

I hesitated, sniffing. The odor was rather pleasant than otherwise, spicy as though it were some form of liqueur. When I touched a drop of it to my tongue, the flavor confirmed this diagnosis. So genial a beverage could hardly be dangerous. And after all, he believed me a fellow student of Roger Bacon. I seated myself in the one chair the room afforded, and sipped.

At once the room and surroundings were blotted out in an immense burst of light, so brilliant that I closed my eyes to shield them from it. When I opened them again, the light was still there all about me, but it seemed to be gathering into me from an outside source, as though my own body were draining it away to leave everything else dark. At the same time there was a wonderful sensation of lightness and freedom.

As my eyes became accustomed to the surrounding dimness, I perceived to my astonishment that I was no longer in the room. There was no trace of a room; I was out under the winter sky, floating along over the lights of New York like a cloud. Beneath and behind me a long trail of phosphorescence like a comet's tail led back to the roof of one of the buildings, I supposed that from which I had come. It was not a hallucination; I have been over New York in a plane, and everything was in the right position and right proportions. I was actually seeing New York from the air; but that phosphorescent trail held me like a tether, I could not get free from it, nor go farther. I felt someone touching my hand, and as the light around me seemed to burn down, there was another flash, and I was back in the room.

The old man with the long hands was smiling into my face.

'An experience, is it not?' he said. 'You did not drink enough to gain the full effect. Would you care to try again? Mandragoreum is not easy to make, but I have enough for you.'

This time I tilted my head back and took a long pull from the flask.

Again the unbearable flash of light, a sense of swift motion. When I opened my eyes, New York City was far beneath, receding into the distance as I seemed to gather speed. The long cord of light that had bound me to the room trailed off behind me; but either its farther end became so small as to be invisible or I had taken enough of the drug altogether to break the connection. In the single glance backward that my speed allowed, I could not even tell toward what part of the city it led.

Clear and bright as I rose, Venus hung like a lamp against the vault of the sky. If I could direct my course, I decided it would be thither, to the most mysterous of the planets. Old Friar Bacon had promised that his drug would 'let hys spirit vade ... toe many a straunge and horrid earthe beyond the bounds of ocean,' and surely Venus met such a definition better than any other place.

I looked back. The earth seemed to be beneath me, fading to a black ball, on which land and sea were just barely visible in the darkness. My speed was still mounting. Suddenly I reached the limit of the earth's shadow; the sun flashed blazingly from behind it, and I beheld the skies as no one on earth has ever seen them – except perhaps Roger Bacon. The nearer planets stood out like so many phases of the moon against the intense blackness of space. The moon itself was a tiny crescent, just visible at the outer edge of the sun, on whose huge disk the earth had sunk to a black spot; yet I found that I could bear to look directly into that glare.

When I turned to look ahead again, however, it was as though my sense of direction had shifted. Venus, growing from the size of a moon to that of a great shield of silver, was no longer overhead, but beneath me, and I was diving downward to a whirling, tossing mass of clouds that reflected the sunlight with dazzling brilliance. Now it was a sea of clouds that seemed to take the shape of a bowl; I reached them, cleft the radiant depths, and at once was in a soundless and almost lightless mass of mist, with no knowledge of my direction except that I seemed to be following the straight course that had brought me here.

The cloud-banks lifted behind me, and I experienced a sense of deep disappointment, for below I saw nothing but an endless ocean, heaving slowly under the heavy groundswell and dotted with drops of rain from the clouds I had just left. The planet of mystery was all one vast ocean, then, inhabited by fishes if by anything, and we men of earth were the only intelligent form of life in the solar system, after all.

I found that I could direct my flight by moving my shoulders and arms, but as I soared across the Venerian ocean, my progress was much slower than it had ever been before. I can only explain this now by the fact that much of the sun's light was cut off by the omnipresent clouds. Roger Bacon's drug undoubtedly makes use of some property of light, that form of energy which is so little understood. I do not know what it can be and my scientific friends laugh at the idea.

But that is wandering from my story. At the time, the slowness of this exploratory voyage gave me no special concern, except that it was becoming monotonous until I perceived in the distance a place where the clouds seemed to touch the surface of the sea. I moved toward it; it soon became clear that this was not the clouds coming down but a thin mist rising up like steam from the surface of a patch of land. But what a land!

It was a water-logged swamp, out of which coiled a monstrous vegetation of a sickly yellow hue, quite without any touch of the green of earthly growths. Here were gigantic mushrooms, that must have been twenty or thirty feet tall; long, slender reedlike stems that burst out at the top into spreading tangles of branches; huge fungus growths of bulbous shape, and a vinelike form that twisted and climbed around and over the reed-trees and giant fungi.

There was no clear line where shore and sea met. The swamp began with a tangle of branches reaching out of the ocean and the growths simply became larger and more dense as one progressed. But at last the ground seemed to be rising; I could catch glimpses of something that was not water among the trunks and vines.

It had occurred to me that where there was much abundant vegetable life, there might be something animal, but up to this point I had seen no sign of anything that might move by its own will under the ceaselessly falling rain and raising mist. But at last I caught sight of a growth resembling the round balls of the fungoids, but too large and too regular to be a fungus. I swung my shoulders toward it; it was a huge ball that seemed made of some material harder and more permanent than the vegetation amid which it rose. I circled the ball; at one side, low down, there was the only opening, a door of some sort. It stood open.

I slid in. The room in which I found myself was very dim and my progress was slow. The light was a kind of phosphorescence like that on the sea at night, issuing from some invisible source. I looked round; I was in a vast hall, whose ceiling vaulted upward until it reached a vertical wall at the other end. From the looks of the outside I had not realized that it was so large. There was no other architectural feature in the place save a hole in the center of the floor, set round with a curbing of some sort.

Slanting toward this with some difficulty of movement, I saw that the hole was a wide well, with the sheen of water visible below. Down into this well went a circular staircase, the stairs of which were broad and fitted with low risers.

From behind the vertical wall at the far end, I was conscious of, rather than heard, a confused shouting, and as I drew near to it I saw that it was pierced by several doors, like the one I had entered by, very thick and heavy. These doors bore horizontal rods which I took to be the Venerian equivalent of doorknobs, and over the terminations of the rods were a series of slits which I took to be approximations of keyholes. I do not know of any sight that would have pleased me more at the moment. Something of the order of cavemen could conceivably have set up such a building; savages might have dug the well and lined it with stairs; but only a fairly intelligent and fairly well-civilized form of life would have doors that locked. We were not alone in the solar system after all.

One of the doors toward the end was open; I drifted through. I don't know what I expected to find inside, but what I did find was beyond any expectation. It was another hall, larger if anything than the first, but not as high, since it was roofed over about halfway up. At each corner a circular staircase, with the same wide, low steps as the well ran up to pierce this ceiling.

The room was filled with an endless range of tables, wide and low, like those in a kindergarten. They were composed of a shimmering metal which may very well have been silver, though it may also have been some alloy of which I am ignorant. At these tables, in high-backed chair-like seats of the same metal sat rows of – the people of Venus. They were busy eating and talking together, like a terrestrial crowd in a busy cafeteria, and their babble was the noise I had sensed.

The Venerians bore a cartoonist's resemblance to seals. They had the same short, barrel-like body, surmounted by the same long, narrow head, but the muzzle had grown back to a face and the forehead was high enough to contain a brain of at least the size of our own. The nostrils were wide and very high, so that the eyes were almost behind them. There were no outer ears, but a pair of holes, low down and toward the back, I took to be orifices for hearing.

The legs of the Venerians are pillar-like muscular appendages, short and terminating in flat, spiny feet, webbed between the four toes. I may mention here that while swimming they trail these feet behind them, using them both for propulsion and changes of direction.

The greatest shock was to see their arms – or rather, the

appendages that served them for arms, since they really had no arms at all. Instead there were tentacles in groups; two groups beginning at the place where the short, thick neck joined the trunk, on the sides, and a third, smaller set springing from the center of the back, high up. These tentacles reached nearly to the floor when a full-grown Venerian was standing at his height of nearly four feet. Each of the three groups contained four tentacles; all the tentacles were prehensile and capable of independent action, giving the Venerian not only an excellent grip on anything, but also the power of picking up as many as twelve objects at a time. I am inclined to think that the tentacles at the back were less functional than the rest; only once did I see a Venerian use one of them.

The Venerians in the hall were entirely innocent of clothing, and all were covered with rough, coarse hair, except for their faces, and of course, the tentacles. Most of them were wearing a type of bandolier, or belt, supported by a strap around the neck, and in turn carrying a series of pocket-like pouches, held shut by clasps. When a Venerian wished to open one, he thrust two of his tentacles into slits in the clasps; I do not know how they operated.

Some of them carried weapons in their belts; short spears or knife-blades, with the handles set T-shape for better grasping in Venerian tentacles. There were also what I later found to be explosive weapons, with a tube springing out from the T-shaped handle. Every tool and weapon was of metal; clearly there could be little wood in this world where the clouds were never broken.

The Venerians were eating with little metal spades, sharpened at the outer end for cutting. Their food came up to them from beneath, through the tables, when they pulled handles set in front of them. The food itself seemed to be the same throughout the hall, some kind of stew, with solids floating in sauces.

I had come in to find the meal nearly over, with Venerians all over the room rising to leave the table and move down the hall with quick, shambling steps. I followed a pair of the weapon-bearers who were talking animatedly together. They went straight to the door into the other hall, crossed it to the well, which they descended till they were about waist-deep, then turned suddenly and dived. I hesitated, then followed; in my envelope of light there was no sense of wetness, and below I found the well turning into a long underwater passage, lit by the same dim radiance that illuminated the hall.

The dimness made it difficult for me to keep up with the Venerians, who were evidently water-livers as we are creatures of the land, for they were amazing swimmers. Abruptly the passage widened, and the light became stronger enough for me to catch up with the pair ahead.

They directed their course upward through the water, came to the surface (where I saw we were well beyond the swamp belt) and took fresh gulps of air through their elevated nostrils. Then, diving beneath the surface again, they coasted along slowly. I caught a flash of something silvery ahead in the water. So did the Venerians. One of them snatched the tube-weapon from his belt, the other jerked out his spear; both swam faster.

Their quarry was a huge fish, its head and body covered with scaly plates. A long tail projected backward from this coat of mail and two big paddles hung near the beast's head. I'm no biologist, but I just happen to have taken my girl to the museum one afternoon, and we saw something just like it. I remember kidding about the tag, which described it as an 'ostracoderm.'

It had seen the Venerians, and evidently had a well-developed respect for them, for it fled down the watery path like an arrow – but not fast enough.

The Venerian with the spear gained more rapidly than his companion, heading the fish off with its barbed point, and herding it round. The other lifted his tubed weapon; there were two muffled thuds, like the blows of a padded hammer, and the seven-foot fish wavered, then stopped, its paddles moving convulsively. The Venerian with the spear ranged alongside, dodged the reflex swing of the long tail, and thrust his weapon in where the bony plate of the head met the cuirass of the body. The big fish heaved once more, then slowly began to sink, but the two Venerians, each wrapping his tentacles round the fish's tail, began to tow him back toward the hall of the well.

Neither of them rose to the surface during all this period. They were marvelously adapted to staying under water.

They were evidently regular, professional hunters by the manner in which they went about their business. It occurred to me that a race which could divide labor in this fashion, which could produce the explosive weapons, and organize life with the ingenuity shown in the common dining-hall, with its ingenious arrangements for service of food, must possess other and interesting establishments of some kind in the swampy land that represented continents on this planet.

Filled with a desire to see them, I took to the air once more and hurried back to the building. The door was still open, and the hall held an assortment of Venerians, some merely standing and talking, some diving into the well to swim off somewhere, and some passing through the portal out into the jungle of fungi. I had seen the sea-hunters; now I followed a party of those who remained on the surface.

They blinked as the brighter light of the out-of-doors struck their eyes, and I wondered what they would do in the dazzling illumination of an earthly day. After a moment or two to accustom their eyes to the light, they struck out up the gentle slope behind the ball-shaped building. The vegetation was a perfect tangle, and I wondered how the Venerians would manage if they left the path they were following until I saw one of them blunder against the trunk of one of the yellow trees. It was all of twenty-five feet high, but his impact sent it crashing to the ground as though it were made of tissue-paper.

The slope became steeper as the Venerians pushed on, kicking the big, soft stems out of their way when they had fallen to block the path. At last the track encountered a buttress of outcropping stone, the first I had seen on the planet. The Venerians paused. Two of them produced tube-weapons from their belts and, walking with some care, took the lead in the group, which had suddenly grown silent.

What were they afraid of? Some grisly amphibian monster of the swamps, I fancy. At all events, one of them suddenly lifted his weapon and fired it in among the crowding growths. I caught a glimpse of a pair of huge eyes, heard the thud of the fall of a big mushroom and that was all. The Venerians with the weapons crouched and peered; there were a few words, and then they pushed on again. On that steaming planet, the ordinary individual must live far closer to the terrors of the beast-world than he does on earth.

The Venerians followed their path down a little dip till it ended at another bulbous building like the hall of the food and the well. Its door was open; within it had the same cold and feeble illumination as the other. All about the outer room of this place were shelves filled with tools, and a Venerian in attendance. At the back another of the thick doors gave on a room in which I glimpsed pulsating machinery. They were that high up the scale.

The party I had followed received tools from the attendant in the outer hall, and came out again, following another path to the hillside behind. There, where a cliff towered out of the swamp, they entered a hole that had been dug in the stony face of the hill, and drawing from the pouches at their belts some balls that emitted the same light I had seen indoors, they plunged in.

I followed them. It was injudicious, no doubt, but I only found that out later. At the time, I had only noticed that my movements were sometimes faster, sometimes slower, and I had not worked out the rationale of what turned out to be a very dangerous business. It also turned out to be an interesting business, though one that had no particular meaning for me, and has not had since.

It was a mine. The Venerians worked it by means of a shafted tool, which is attached by a metal cord to a box about two feet square, the box standing on the floor behind the miner and evidently furnishing the power for the operation. At the working end of the shafted head is a circle of metal teeth, and beneath the teeth a basket of woven metal. The Venerian presses the tool against the rock he is mining. The teeth spring into motion with the pressure, the rock is pulverized and falls into the basket as a powder. When the basket is filled, the miner takes it to the power box, empties it in and pulls a small rod. Immediately, the box emits a strong red glow, and in a minute or two a bar of shining metal is discharged at the back, and a little ball of waste material falls beside it.

When a pile of the metal bars has accumulated, the miner picks them up and carries them back to the tool-hall, where he turns them in, receiving in exchange a metal token which he deposits in one of his pouches.

I watched the Venerian miners carefully and for a long while, hoping to learn the secret of their power box. Eventually, I thought, something would go wrong with one of them, or it would need a re-charge, and the miner would open it. If I could get an inkling of that, and tell it to some of my engineering friends, it would not only be proof of my strange experience, but it might also be worth – well, a great deal.

So much interested in the project did I become, that I failed to notice the passage of time, and during one of the miner's visits to the hall of the machines, as I waited for him to return, I suddenly realized that it had grown dark. The miner, too, seemed to be gone for an extraordinarily long time. If he had finished his assigned task for the day, there was no sense remaining where I was. I started to leave – and found I could not move an inch.

It was at this point I realized the implications of the fact that Roger Bacon's drug enabled the use of the power of light. There was no light; and there I was, bound by motionlessness, as though in a nightmare; marooned on a planet millions of miles from home, from my own body even, and with no means of returning. I could hear the crash of some beast through the vegetation and the patter of the eternal Venerian rain. That was all; I was alone.

At such moments, in spite of the statements of some writers, one does not rave and storm, or review the mistakes of a past life. I thought of my body back in the room on Bank Street, Earth, and what the old man would do as it sat there in the chair, lifelessly. Would he dare to call the police or a doctor? Would he try to dispose of part of 'me'? Was there any antidote to the drug mandragoreum that he could apply? Suppose I finally obtained some kind of release, with the coming of the Venerian dawn, and came rushing home to find my body beneath the waters of the Hudson or on a dissecting table in the New York morgue?

Or perhaps I would remain as a disembodied brain there on Venus throughout eternity? The creatures of this planet had taken no notice of me, and I had made no attempt to communicate with them. Could I if I wished? It was a pretty academic problem. I remembered Jack London's remark that the blackest thing in nature was a hole in a box. That was what I was in – a hole in a box.

From that point, I turned to wondering how long it would be before dawn on Venus. For all I knew it might not come for fifty or sixty hours – quite enough time for anything on earth to happen to my body. It would begin to need nourishment, even if nothing more drastic happened to it. There it sat, in what resembled a hypnotic trance. How long could people stay alive in such a state? I tried to remember and could not recall ever having heard anywhere. Every time I tried to review my knowledge on the subject it turned out to be too sketchy to be helpful.

I was aroused from this reverie by a grunting sound like that made by a wallowing pig, and looking toward the mouth of the cave, saw a pair of phosphorescent eyes gleaming at the entrance. Apparently the animal, who had no outline in that absolute black, was disturbed by the smell of the place, for the grunts changed into a grinding bellow and it backed out. Perhaps I could communicate with the Venerians after all – provided my mind did not die with my distant body.

Followed another series of grunts, and the sound of heavy footsteps, followed by angry snarls. Then came the sound of heavy bodies hurled about. Two of the Venerian beasts were fighting outside my prison. Of all the events of that journey, this one stands out most clearly; the quarrel of those two Venerian monsters, whose shape I did not even know, snarling and biting each other under the rain, while I hung in the cave without the power of motion.

The battle trailed off to one side and ended in grunting moans, which in turn faded into a sound suggestive of eating. One of the invisible beasts had evidently been victorious and was celebrating – noisily. Finally this sound also ceased, and there was only the steady beat of the rain.

It seemed to grow heavier, and I began to wonder how that mattered on a planet where it was always raining. Far in the distance, I heard the roll of thunder; and I noted without really thinking about it that they had thunderstorms on Venus as well as earth.

The rain fell harder; again came the peal of thunder, and as it rolled I could see lightning flickering, far in the distance. A new, wild hope rose in me. Lightning was light; if one of those flashes came near enough —

For a time it seemed that it would not. The lightning flashed away among the distant clouds, the thunder continued to boom, but the storm seemed about to pass off to one side and away from me. I was just giving up hope when there were simultaneously a terrific crash and a dazzling burst of lightning across the door of the cave.

With a twist of the shoulders, I was out and riding. It was as dark as before out there, but I was now in the open, where I could travel on any flash of lightning that came, and I did, in a long series of jerking leaps. Another flash – I was among the clouds. Another – I was more than halfway through them. I believed I could see the stars of space beyond. Another flash below me, and I was at last out of the atmosphere of that grim and slimy planet and riding the ether in the light of the stars.

When I reached the earth and the room on Bank Street, dawn was just coming up behind the skyscrapers. I felt cold and numb all over; the old man was standing in the center of the room, looking at me anxiously.

'Thank God!' he said, as I opened my eyes and moved a palsied hand. 'I had begun to fear that you could not make the return trip, and I would have to look for you – although that is very difficult for a person of my constitution.'

'I need some coffee,' was all I said; and as I looked at him, I noticed how very much he resembled the Venerians I had seen.

'Was it an interesting journey?' he asked.

'Wonderful; but I need some coffee,' I repeated. 'I'll tell you about it later.'

I staggered out and down the stairs. And that's just the trouble about my story. There wasn't any later.

For after I fumbled through a day's work at the bank, I got to thinking about things, and I wasn't quite sure whether I wanted to go back there again alone; that is, until I had talked to someone else about it. When I did summon up nerve enough to go back, a couple of evenings later, I found there wasn't any name beside the top button in the row in the hall, and nobody answered the bell when I rang. So I pushed the button marked 'Super' and a fat woman with scraggly hair came out.

As I remarked before, I didn't even know the old man's name. 'Who lives on the top floor?' I asked.

'Nobody,' she said. 'Not now, anyway.' She gave me a suspicious look. 'If you're another one of them G-men, I want to see your badge.'

So there it is. I went away. I'm not a G-man. I don't want them looking for me when I have to work in a bank. It could be that the old man gave me some kind of dope, and that he was mixed up in the racket somehow. I don't know. But if he was, why did he have all those old rolls of sheepskin up there? They were genuine, all right. And any scientific people I've talked to since say that my description of Venus is just about what it would look like. Me, I just don't know.

Smoke of the Snake

CARL JACOBI

HERRICK ARRIVED in Samarinda at night when it was late enough for him to slip unnoticed by the strict and watchful Dutch immigration authorities and sufficiently dark to remove all chances of detection by the native police.

He groped his way cautiously across the worm-eaten wharves, moved slowly with a familiar step through the evil-smelling blackness of the water front, and headed toward a line of distant street lights that glimmered like yellow eyes in the fog.

Borneo again – no different than it had been three years before. Kuching, Bandjermasin, Samarinda – they were all the same. Brooding, mysterious, rat-infested coastal towns, fever holes cut from the dark clutches of the jungle, populated by a few white men and the dregs of the Eastern circle.

Herrick drew up at the outskirts of the illuminated area, stepped into the doorway shadow of a steel-walled copra warehouse, lit a cigarette, and swore in disgust.

He was ship-tired, hungry, and thirsty. More than that, his nerves at the present moment were near the breaking point. Six months' intermittent enjoyment with the powers of the poppy were not to be disregarded, and he hadn't had a single pipe of opium since the day he left Makassar.

His need was desperate.

He waited until the street before him was deserted, then shuffled slowly forward, heading not toward the European quarter – too dangerous there – but deep into the winding, crooked alleys of the native sector.

As he walked he peered carefully at each darker building shadow, hung his right hand, unswinging, close to the pocket of his duck coat. The slight bulge there marked the presence of an easily accessible automatic, loaded with a full clip and ready for instant action. A man – even a man on the right side of the law – needed a gun in this sinister spiderweb, and Herrick with a 'wanted' sign hung out for him by both the British and Dutch governments and a price on his head in every port south of Sandakan, was not unaware of his perilous position.

A line of sordid shops, all identically the same, with drooling, half-darkened windows, slipped by him into the gloom. Herrick smiled grimly.

Old stamping grounds, these. He remembered it all. But he had sunk pretty low since he had walked by here in a fresh suit of whites and Pollyanna ideas about the East. He had gone down into the very gutter and he had changed a lot, mentally as well as physically. He felt the heavy stubble on his face, ran his fingers across the ragged scar that marred his left cheek, and looked down at his torn and filthy clothes. No, there was no danger of his being recognized. Even Liang Po wouldn't know him, and Liang Po's was his destination.

He found the place presently, sunk in that forbidding by-street with its mongrel half-English, half-Chinese sign.

It was the Liang Po's of old. No change. The same tobacco-filled air, the same rough tables, the same confusion of black, brown, and bleary white faces. A reed flute wailed above the rhythmic cadence of a pounded drum, and in a farther corner a Dyak dancing girl, clad only in breast plates and skirt of beads, whirled and swayed in wild abandon.

Herrick chose a table away from the others, pushed back his sun helmet, and relaxed in the chair.

Half an hour later he was still sitting there, a bottle of whisky and a dish of sour-smelling rice mixture half consumed. He swept the bottle and dish aside presently, took out a deck of greasy cards, and began to lay them on the table.

'The white stranger would be interested, perhaps, in buying a bit of opium?'

Herrick started, jerked his hand toward his automatic pocket, and looked up. Before him, round face smiling, almond eyes half closed like some drowsing Buddha, sat a small, ancient Chinese. His face was crossed and crisscrossed with a thousand wrinkles, and his hand, as he laid it delicately on the table, looked like a withered claw.

For a moment Herrick stared in silence. He knew that to one familiar with the signs the ravages of the drug which he had resorted to with increasing frequency were plainly written in his jaundiced complexion and the sunken hollows behind his ears. He knew, too, that he looked different, a lot different. Three years was a long time. Yet the slit eyes of the Oriental seemed to see beyond all physical changes, to probe his very soul.

'You are—' Herrick asked, nervously lighting a cigarette.

'Liang Po. I sell what others buy. You want opium?'

Herrick did not lower his guard. He shuffled the deck of cards slowly, cut them, and shuffled again. He laid his cigarette on the edge of the table, exhaled a last streamer of smoke, and deliberately studied the withered face before him.

'Make it strong,' he said at length. 'I've been without the stuff so long I can't see straight.'

Without another word Liang Po rose, motioned Herrick to follow, and led the way through a mat-covered doorway into a dark and sickly-sweet-smelling corridor. Lighted by a flaring rag in a dish of oil, the corridor extended deep into the shadows, and there were many closed doors along each side wall.

Before one of these the Chinese stopped, drew from his robes a key, and inserted it in the lock.

'Enter,' he said shortly. Herrick, stepping across the threshold, found himself in a small low-ceilinged room. There was a couch covered with silken drapes, a table of teakwood, and a curious triangular cabinet fashioned of colored bamboo which rested on a base of ivory.

'White man,' said the Oriental softly, seating himself on the couch, 'it is true, is it not, that you have wished many times that you had never succumbed to the habit of the opium pipe?'

'Wished?' Herrick dug his fingers into his palms convulsively. Lord, how much truth there was in the words! A thousand times he had cursed the folly of that day when he had first introduced himself to the drug. He hated the stuff, hated to think it was slowly strengthening its grip on him, gradually writing his death sentence. He paced forward a few steps, head down, then whirled, gritting his teeth.

'I can pay,' he snapped. 'Don't sit there like a gaping idiot. What the hell are you waiting for?'

Liang Po's face was inscrutable as he reached sideways into the little bamboo cabinet next to the couch, opened a panel at its top, and drew two articles from its interior. A long tubelike something, curved like a serpent, and a small lacquer box.

'Suppose,' he said, 'I were to offer you a drug of a different nature, one which, chemically speaking, contains neither morphine, thebaine, nor papaverine; a substance which —'

Herrick shook his head. 'Hashish? Charas?' he said. 'Nothing doing. Opium is bad enough for me.'

'But no, my friend. I speak of something entirely different, something which as a white man you have never heard of before.'

Liang Po opened the lacquer box and shook into his palm five green pellets. They were oblong, Herrick noted, the size of quinine capsules, five grain, and they seemed to glow and glisten like oil on water when the light from the flickering lantern struck their surfaces.

'Two of these pellets smoked in this curved pipe, and you will drowse in beautiful dreams. Dreams which put the opium stupor to shame. Three pellets, and the joys of heaven will fly down to you. You will be an emperor in the realm of sleep with the world whirling strangely in a circle of happiness. And when you awaken, all desire, all urge, for the taste of opium will have gone into the rising smoke.'

Herrick started as though prodded with a knife.

'You mean,' he gasped, 'you mean – that that stuff is an antidote, a cure for —'

Liang Po's wrinkled face moved closer under the lantern light like a grinning gargoyle.

'I mean that after breathing its fumes the drug of the poppy will have no more effect upon you than a bowl of rice. The pipe comes from Soerabaya, from the limb of a Upas tree. It is said two men lost their lives removing the *antjar* juice from its core and fashioning it into its present form. But the pellets – you have been far enough into the interior jungles to have seen that most evil of snakes, the hamadryad? And to know the deadly poison it carries in its fangs?'

Herrick nodded slowly.

'These pellets contain that poison. They were made in a native kampong, far up the Mahakam River. Made by Kajan Dyaks, compounded under the direction of Lukut, and Lukut is a witch doctor, an all-seeing man of many secrets.

'On a night when the moon is at the full and the tabu of the rice feast forgotten, a live hamadryad is thrown into a kettle of boiling blood, blood which is drained from the body of a young Dyak girl. Into the mixture are thrown the teeth of nine crocodiles and the skull of a female orang-utan. The potion is stirred with a golden parang – slowly, and the scum spooned off and allowed to dry. It is ground to a powder then and blended with the thorn of the *klubi*, the swamp plant which —'

'You, a Chinese, believe in these native superstitions?' broke in Herrick.

Liang Po shrugged. 'I follow the religion of my ancestors,' he said. 'But I was born here in Samarinda, and I also believe what I have seen to be true.'

Herrick was thinking fast. It would be the height of absurdity to insert in his system a mixture the nature of which he didn't know. Made from the virus of a hamadryad – smoked through a pipe of poisonous Upas wood! And yet harmless enough because of the sorcery of a jungle witch doctor.

Well, he had wandered through the East long enough to know that things happened here which never found a place in the pages of a medical journal. If the stuff were a cure for the opium habit — Good God, if it really were!

He glanced down at the Oriental's lacquer box and then at his own trembling hands. A cure would wipe away that itching desire that was driving him mad. A cure would —

He stood there, gnawing his lips, staring blankly into space.

And softly, silkily Liang Po's droning voice continued:

'The curious thing about these pellets, white man, is that, when smoked in this pipe, no two will superinduce the same type of dreams. One time you will be living again some happy hours of the past. Again, the mysteries of the future will be revealed to you. Or perhaps —'

'Never mind that,' snapped Herrick. 'Are you sure the drug will take away all desire for opium? If you're lying to me —'

'I am not lying, white man. I speak the truth. My pellets come from the deep jungle country, brought downriver once a year. No one else in Samarinda has them.'

Herrick shut his teeth decisively. He reached in his pocket and threw several coins to the table.

'Fill the pipe and get out,' he said. 'I'll try anything once.'

Without haste Liang Po rose to his feet, pushed two of the pellets into the bowl of the pipe, and laid the remaining three on the table. The lacquer box he returned to the bamboo cabinet.

'Taken correctly,' he said to Herrick, 'there is no danger in the drug. Two pellets the first time. After that any number up to four. But on your life do not use the fifth. It will cause a constriction of the heart, and you will die in torture.'

He went out, closing the door behind him. Herrick stood

there in the silence, gazing down at the pipe on the table, brow twisted in a frown. The thing was a lot different from any *yensheegow* he had ever smoked, that was certain. It was carved and colored into a perfect likeness of a brown snake. Even the mouthpiece, long and slender, was fashioned like a protruding fang.

With an involuntary shudder Herrick picked the pipe up and brought it closer to examine the crushed remnants of the two pellets in the bowl. For a moment, then, he imagined the greenish powder was swirling round and round, coiled and wriggling as though alive. Then he jerked his eyes away and reached in his pocket for a match. It was getting him already, that opium desire, eating into his vitals in a way that smothered all reluctance. In a few months that urge would be greater, a hundred times greater. And it would increase quickly until life would be a torture. He had seen addicts in the last stages many times. They shuffled along the streets like moving corpses with their palms turned to the rear and their coats draped over their shoulders like capes. And they knew the use of the *sueypow*, the knife with which the degraded scrapes the bowl of the pipe, and then eats those scrapings.

Slowly Herrick applied the match, stretched full length on the couch, and let the smoke pass down the stem into his mouth. For a while there was no reaction, only a strange half-sweet, half-bitter taste that tingled like a hundred needles far back in his throat. He expelled the smoke and watched it rise in thin, greenish coils toward the darkness of the ceiling. It seemed to gather there in a compact cloud, that smoke, hang motionless like a roll of transparent cloth. And then drowsiness and a feeling of quiet stole over the white man, and he closed his eyes while the silence of the room drew in about him.

If he were asleep, it was sleep such as he had never experienced. Vaguely he was aware of the steady pulsation of his heart and the pipe through which he continued to inhale the fumes from the burning pellets. The effect of the smoke was delightful now. It coursed through his veins in a subdued electric glow, and it produced a sense of warmth that penetrated his brain like old wine.

Body relaxed, muscles untensed, Herrick lay there, gradually drawing deeper and deeper on the pipe. Under the lids of his closed eyes he could see the smoke cloud directly above him grow from a small, translucent billow the size of a palm frond to a thick blanket that reached from wall to wall. It continued to increase in size as the exhalations from the man's mouth and the pungent incense from the bowl of the pipe rose upward.

How much time elapsed after that Herrick did not know. But when he suddenly found himself staring, eyes wide open, at the farther wall, a curious thing had happened.

The wall, once so solid and material, had passed away, and in its place was a scene that stretched far beyond, a gallery with carven balustrades continuing and perspectively diminishing almost to the vanishing point. The floor and the ceiling were vague and indistinct with the kaleidoscopic unreality of a Goya drawing, but the brown balusters, illumined from above by a curious indefinable glow, existed with a sharpness and a clarity as though seen through a magnifying glass. And extending from the very corner of Herrick's eye to the remoteness before him was that strange greenish smoke, diffused now, wafting slowly from side to side like an entity restless and alive.

An instant later, confused and bewildered, Herrick was advancing forward into the length of the gallery. He had no remembrance of leaving the couch or of passing from the mundane reality of the little room. He only knew that in some inexplicable manner he was being drawn toward the mystery of what lay ahead, urged on by a magnetic force. His feet moved with the unhurried, precise steps of a follower of a funeral cortege, and his hands hung rigid at his sides.

Keeping well to the center of the geometric plane, Herrick continued his mechanical pace, his brain seeking frantically for something which it could understand. On and on he went, never altering his step. His nostrils were dry and glazed from the continuous inhalation of smoke, and his lungs felt hard and swollen, as though some bulbous substance had crawled down his wind pipe and increased in size.

He came in this manner to the end of the gallery. Here the way before him merged into a grand staircase that swept down to a level far below. One moment Herrick hesitated, fighting the attraction that was drawing him so relentlessly; then slowly he began to descend.

Below him was a circular platform, large as an arena, seeming to hang suspended on the dark billows like a floating island. The floor was white, a dazzling white, made all the more intense by the heavy blackness that surrounded it on three sides. He reached the last step and emerged upon it. Not until then did Herrick have an undistorted vision of his surroundings, and he gazed before him with eyes full of utter amazement.

Directly ahead the smoke had gathered and then divided itself into three distinct segments, three towering, separate mist columns. They were but thicker coagulations of the greenish fumes, wavering and translucent, yet in a dim, uncertain way they possessed human form and appearance. And suddenly as though moulded by an invisible sculptor, details developed, features grew, and three nebulous, lifelike images stood motionless and erect before him.

One instant Herrick surveyed them, examined their heads and bodies. Then he recoiled while a slow chill crawled its way along his spine.

On the left, feet braced far apart, seaman's cap pulled well back from his brow, was the likeness of a ship captain, heavily bearded, with little pig eyes and huge loose jowls.

The second figure of the tenuous triad was a Chinese girl, delicate and beautiful in spite of its size, as any Tanagra figurine.

And the third —

Herrick stared at the third image. The vapor statue was a perfect effigy of himself; not himself as he looked at the present time, wasted by narcotics, roughened by a life spent in every hole of the East, but himself with the clean suit of whites, the spotless pith helmet, and the clear eyes he had had when he first set foot in Samarinda three years before.

For many moments the triple figure-piece mirage remained there, unreal yet stereoscopically distinct. Then, like a darkened reflection, it disintegrated again, and there were only the heavy greenish fumes swirling languidly from side to side.

Herrick, watching it, had felt like a man alone in outer space watching a dimensional drama through the lanes of time. Now, however, with the vision gone before him, he suddenly turned his eyes toward the murky background that hung like a curtain beyond the platform. And what he saw brought a scream of terror bursting from his throat.

That background, that misty darkness which surrounded the illumined area, was an undulating blanket of horror. Out there, wriggling, crawling, crossed and interwoven like the design of some colossal tapestry, was a compact mass of snakes – small snakes, large snakes, flat-headed and alive. They were watching him, Herrick saw, watching him with a thousand pairs of eyes. and they were advancing slowly nearer.

With a choking cry Herrick turned and lunged for the staircase, the only way he knew of escape. But his limbs seemed held back by some unseen weight, some power which permitted him to advance only at a measured, deliberate pace. A cold numbness seized him, penetrated to his very brain, and he worked at the stairs like a madman.

Behind him he could hear a mighty hissing and rustling as the horde of slime-surrounded serpents twisted and writhed and sought to free themselves from their own entangling folds, sought to reach the prey in their path. It was a jellylike wall, wavering and gelatinous, and the snakes existed within it as though cast from some giant mold. They were cobras, all of them, brown, squirming lengths of horror, hooded, with bluish-white under portions. Like flowing lava they moved across the floor of the platform.

Then it happened. Before he could flail his arms forward,

before he could throw his weight to the side, Herrick's legs buckled under him, and he fell sprawling, face to the floor, He screamed, shot a frantic glance over his shoulder, strained every effort to rise from the psychic encumbrance that was overwhelming him.

But, like a man in a hypnotic trance, he found himself powerless to move. And with a slow and inexorable movement the snake mass crossed the intervening distance, and, cold and clinging, began to slide its coils over his body.

Exactly what happened after that Herrick could not be sure. The scene faded – abruptly and completely. The grand staircase, the gallery above, and the overpowering horror all diffused into nothingness, and once more he was lying on the silken couch flanked by the material walls of the little room.

Drunkenly he rose to his feet, flung the strange Upas pipe to a far corner.

'What vile stuff!' he gasped. Then, coughing and retching, he stumbled to the door and went out.

It was the night of the following day, and Liang Po sat at one of the corner tables of his drink shop surveying through half-closed eyes the confusion that surged around him. He sat with a smile on his wrinkled face, contemplating the future, and he did not move until, many moments later, there came the interruption he had been waiting for.

The door leading to the street was ripped open, and a haggard figure lurched into the room. Herrick, clothes wet and soggy from the rain that was pounding Samarinda's streets without, staggered into the chair opposite the Chinese and spread his hands flat on the table.

For a moment he sat there, silent, lips quivering, face a deadly white. Then he caught his breath and leaned forward.

'You lied!' he cried. 'You miserable, double-crossing rat! You told me that drug was a cure for the opium habit! You told me that, didn't you? Answer, or I'll—'

Hands folded, eyes gleaming like two pinpoints of flame, Liang Po studied the man before him.

'I spoke the truth,' he said softly. 'My pellets will release all who smoke them from the powers of the poppy.'

'Release him, yes!' Herrick's voice was choked with bitterness. 'Release him, but bind him stronger than ever to your own devilish concoction! Liang Po, you knew the effect those fumes would have on me once they had entered my system. You knew that they caused insane dreams, more horrible than the wildest imagination. You knew that it was more powerful, more habit-forming than the strongest brand of opium. All day I've felt myself wanting it. All day I've tried to fight it off. It's driving me mad, I tell you! I've got to have another dose!'

The Oriental listened, adjusted the sleeve of his crimson robe, and shook his head in a slow negative.

'No,' he said quietly; 'no more pellets are for sale. The ingredients which compose them are not grown in a field like so much rice. They are difficult to obtain and therefore most costly. I do not sell them at random.'

'But I tell you I've got to have it!'

Without emotion Liang Po gave no heed to the frantic words. He stared across the room at the lithe form of the Dyak dancing girl, watched her as she whirled and swayed and entertained his money-paying guests.

For a moment Herrick hesitated, hands clamped hard against the table edge. He moistened his lips, coughed deep in his throat, twisted in his chair. Then, as he looked into the other's face, he saw something that made him clutch like a drowning man at a last straw.

'There is a price other than money?'

Over on the far side of the room the reed flute continued its wailing sound, and the drums throbbed sullenly. The murmur of the surrounding voices seemed to grow momentarily softer as Liang Po roused himself, moved a few inches closer, and curled his lips in a slow smile.

'There might very well be a price other than money, if you are the kind of a man I think you are. But I am not sure.'

'Meaning —'

'A brave man, white stranger. A man who has learned,

perhaps, not to value too highly the lives of other men when their removal could be of profit to him.'

Herrick squirmed uneasily. 'Spill it,' he said. 'If I don't have more of that dope soon, I'll go crazy.'

Face gleaming in the wavering glare of the bracket lamps like an old Chinese mask, Liang Po was silent while he studied Herrick for a long moment. When he spoke, his lips barely moved, and his voice, passing over the table, was a subdued whisper.

'White man,' he said, 'there is now at the water front of Samarinda a trading ship, a schooner out of Java, called the *Kuala Han*. Her captain is a white man – Sledge Carper – and was once well known in this port.'

Herrick froze. His teeth went together with a sudden click.

'Carper?' he repeated. 'What about him?'

'There is a lot about him, white man. Three years ago this Carper stole my most treasured possession, took it from me as if I were a rat. He kidnapped my only daughter, my little flower girl, Wu. With the aid of another man, whom I have never known, he took her aboard his ship and then sailed away before I learned what had happened.

'Not until many months did I know the truth. Then it was too late. Wu was young and delicate, and Carper a fiend with the body of a gorilla. She died somewhere out there in the Java sea. Carper threw her body overboard and laughed while he did it.'

Herrick was gnawing his finger tips. 'Well?' he asked.

'White man, you have asked for more snake pellets and my pipe. As I have said, both were difficult to obtain and therefore most costly. But the cure will be complete the second time, I am sure. The urge for more will disappear completely.

'My price is not difficult. I want no money. Something far easier. You will steal your way across the wharves, board the *Kuala Han* if necessary, find this Captain Carper – *and kill him!*'

Like a tightened wire Herrick slowly grew rigid in his chair. 'You want me to murder the man?' he said.

The Chinese nodded coldly. 'Sledge Carper has defiled my race and the sacred ashes of my ancestors,' he said.

'He has brought sorrow to my house, and for that he must die.'

'But—'

Liang Po rose to his feet abruptly. 'I have spoken,' he said. 'If you wish more pellets, that is my answer.'

An hour later Herrick made his way through the stench-filled alleys of Samarinda's native quarter toward the heavier darkness of the water front. A slow, penetrating drizzle was falling from a black sky, and the streets were deserted. He reached the docks, skirted bales and boxes and piles of stinking copra, and moved deliberately over the rotten planking toward the farthest extent of the wharves.

A length of darker shadow of familiar size rose up out of the gloom, and the white man muttered in satisfaction. Like an overnourished sea bat, the bulging hulk of a weather-scarred tramp packet lay sprawled there. On her bow in almost illegible lettering was the name *Kuala Han.*

Herrick looked carefully about him; then, satisfied that he hadn't been followed, he dropped behind an empty hogshead, drew from his pocket a long, curved creese, and proceeded to wait.

The *Kuala Han.* He hadn't forgotten her. Chinese-owned, manned by a cutthroat crew, the scum of every port from Penang to Batavia, and captained by 'Sledge' Carper, who, not without reason, had the reputation of being the cruelest skipper in these seas, a six-foot-four carcass of animal lust and brutality.

Now Herrick was going to kill him. Queer, the turns of fate. Three years before, when he had seen less of the black side of life, Herrick would have blanched at the thought of it. He had feared Carper then, had obeyed the man's orders like a whining puppy. It was still clear in his memory, the night the two of them had returned from an hour's carousal at Liang

Po's, and Carper had talked drunkenly, obscenely of the girl he had seen there.

'Her name's Wu, and she's the lousy old chink's daughter. Prettiest little trick I've ever seen, even if she is yellow. I want her, Herrick. The *Kuala Han* ain't had a woman on board for a long time. Go back there and get her. I don't care how. Bring her aboard. If you don't, I'll tell the Dutch officials a few things I know.'

Herrick had obeyed, but he had also been careful. And for that, now, three years later, he thanked his lucky stars. Liang Po knew Carper was responsible for the kidnaping and the subsequent death of his daughter, and he wanted revenge. But he hadn't recognized Herrick in his changed appearance or connected him with the distant crime.

It meant that everything was working nicely for the white man crouching there in the blackness of the docks. It meant that in a few moments Sledge Carper, a man whom he had come to hate with his very life and soul, would be dead and unable to hold over him any longer that little affair of rifle smuggling to upriver natives which had worried Herrick for so long. Kill two birds with one stone, they said. Well, he was killing three. He was getting his own personal revenge, he was destroying a source of possible criminal evidence against him, and in return for all that he was to receive payment from Liang Po in the form of more pellets and another trial at his Upas pipe. A good bargain!

And even if his body ached now as it had ached all the hours since he had quitted the strange, greenish fumes, with a wild desire for more of the snake powder, he felt sure a second smoke would alleviate that feeling entirely. The Chinese had said the pellets were a cure for the opium habit. He had also said desire for the pellets themselves would disappear after the second application. In the first case he had been right. Why should he choose to lie about the latter?

The rain was coming down harder as he crouched there, and Herrick impatiently shifted his position. Below him, hollow and muffled, he could hear the water slapping monotonously against the piles of the dock. Off to the right, far out on the bay, a red dot, the riding light of a junk, glimmered dimly through the murk.

Only one thing worried Herrick – his eyes. They had been acting queerly all day. On three separate occasions he had caught himself staring at objects which apparently floated before him, but which could not by any law of nature actually exist.

Even now, as his eyes looked into it, the darkness seemed porous around him, alive and swirling with tiny pinpoints of light. Ahead in the intervening distance between the protecting hogshead and the silent bulk of the schooner, a lighter glow hung suspended like an optic scar in his vision. He opened and closed his eyes, then swore when the thing did not pass.

It was that face again, the face of Liang Po with its wizened skin and twisted smile. And above it he saw, like a writhing halo, the brown form of a coiled snake.

Imagination, nothing more. It was all an impossibility, a creation of his mind. A man's nerves always played tricks on him when he had been under a strain for any length of time. He shifted his gaze, but the floating face and the snake persisted.

Then abruptly Herrick grasped the handle of the creese harder and tensed like a cat. He had heard approaching footsteps and the sound of heavy breathing. A moment later a bulking figure lurched out of the gloom.

One instant Herrick waited while he made sure the drunken form was that of Sledge Carper. One instant he fastened his eyes on the bearded face, on the towering, apelike body. Then, as the man reeled heavily past, he leaped forward, raised the creese high over his head, and brought it down straight in the back of his victim's neck.

The figure stopped short and stiffened. A single hoarse scream gurgled from his lips. Then the heavy thump of a falling body, and Herrick was racing from the scene, running wildly toward the spiderweb protection of the native sector.

Back in the little room in the rear of the drink shop, Liang Po smiled as he listened.

'You have done well,' he said, 'very well, and the payment I promised shall be yours. The pipe lies on the couch. It is ready for use, and you may smoke it undisturbed. Here on the table are five pellets.'

The Chinese moved toward the door, leaving Herrick standing in the middle of the room, fingers trembling with anticipation.

'I ask you to remember only one thing, white man,' he added. 'Use only four pellets. No more. Four may be taken without danger, but the fifth means —'

Herrick was not listening. Arms extended before him, he was advancing unsteadily toward the pipe. He would smoke the thing once more, get rid of that damnable urge, and then he would clear out of here, leave Borneo for good. There was Papua. No one would know him there, and he could always make his way by hook or crook. He would forget this sordid past and start anew.

There was no hesitation in his actions now. Feverishly he pushed two of the pellets into the pipe bowl and left the remaining three on the table. Feverishly he dug in his pockets for a match, lit it, stretched full length on the couch, and inserted the fanglike mouthpiece between his lips.

And over on the far side of the room Liang Po smiled as he stepped across the threshold.

'Only four pellets,' he said softly, closing the door behind him. 'No more.'

A moment later, as the fumes began to creep slowly down his lungs, Herrick closed his eyes in satisfaction. It was happening the same as before. The same feeling of internal warmth and pleasure, the same electric glow reaching deep into the core of his brain.

But his dreams that night were different. They were a succession of realistic scenes, a chronological panorama of his immediate past.

He saw himself as an upstanding official taking his tiffin in a clean, white-roomed house in the European quarter. He saw the first step of his downfall, a sampan moored at the river jetty, loaded with rifles for upriver natives and for which he was to receive much money. He saw his meeting with Sledge Carper and his part in the kidnaping of Wu, Liang Po's daughter. Events of the subsequent three years hurried by then in a swiftly moving state of confusion. Events that in most cases were not pleasant: stealings, swindlings, murder over a game of fan tan in Kuching, and endless pursuit by the British and Dutch police.

Hours seemed to have passed when Herrick opened his eyes and stared once more at the walls around him. The pipe had gone out, the pellets in the bowl were consumed, but the greenish smoke still hung like an emerald pall a few inches below the ceiling. Throughout his entire body there was growing a mighty urge, a wild desire to taste more of the strange drug. He could not resist it.

Dazedly Herrick struggled to his feet, lurched across to the teak table, and stared at the remaining pellets on the surface. A moment he stood there, while the lantern in the far corner flickered and flared and trembled his shadow before him. Then he filled the pipe again, returned to the couch, and began to suck wildly at the sweetish fumes that he craved.

Above him, he could see through the blur of his half-closed lashes the smoke cloud grow thicker and thicker and begin to swirl gently from side to side. And then once more the opposite wall faded like a darkened picture, and in its place there appeared that vast endless gallery extending straight as a geometric line to the vanishing point.

Herrick was watching it with a curious sense of familiarity. The scene was the same, the brown, carven balustrades, the indistinct floor and ceiling, and the strange glow that illumined the expanse with the vagueness of light through water.

But suddenly the white man became rigid on the couch. He blinked his eyes, stared, looked again, studied the scene before him while a cold chill edged its way up his spine. Slowly,

slowly advancing down the center of the gallery, moving upon the billows of greenish vapor, was an object that filled his very soul with horror.

It was a hamadryad – a King Cobra!

Wriggling, sliding, with its hooded head outthrust before it, it was approaching the confines of the little room. Herrick tensed his muscles and sought frantically to rise from the

couch; but, as before, that psychic heaviness seemed to have overwhelmed him, and he found himself powerless to move.

Inch by inch the serpent came on, at times seeming to merge with the swirling fumes, at times sharp and clear as an engraved design. There was a relentlessness in its advance, a slow, nightmare persistence that struck at the very sockets of the white man's eyes. And presently it had emerged from the gallery, entered the room, and was hanging directly over the couch, suspended in the vapor cloud.

Herrick lay there motionless as though bound in chains. He saw the snake as through a telescope, brown on top, bluish white underneath, with black, gleaming eyes. He watched the fangs stab the heavy air, whip back and forth hungrily.

And suddenly he saw that the green vapor was slowly diffusing and the snake was settling toward him.

Frantically the white man sucked on the pipe and began to expel huge clouds of smoke toward the descending horror. For it was those fumes alone that seemed to buoy it in mid-air above him. He smoked until his mouth was on fire, until his lungs ached deep in his chest and the room was thick with the dense miasma.

Only an instant the hamadryad hesitated. Then it gathered its coils under it – poised – and dropped swiftly downward.

A long time later Liang Po opened the door and silently entered the room. He moved across to the couch and stared down upon the silent figure that lay upon it. Smiling, he released the pipe from the stiffened fingers and returned it to its bamboo cabinet. And he was still smiling when he stepped again to the door and cast a last look behind him.

For the dull surface of the teak table was empty now. The fifth pellet was no longer there.

Melodramine

HENRY SLESAR

My fingernails dug into concrete as I clung to the narrow ledge 30 stories above Fifth Avenue. It was a windless night, thank God; the slightest breeze off the river would have blown me into eternity. Somehow, I negotiated my way to the next window and managed to kick out the glass with my heel; the pane shattered in big, shiny pieces. I almost cried with relief once I was inside and saw that by some miracle I had crashed my own apartment. A second later, I knew there was no worse place to be that night. Questikian would be waiting for me.

'Welcome home.' His too familiar voice sounded sibilant no matter what the words. 'Nice of you to drop in.'

'Bad joke,' I snarled. 'Bad joke, Questikian, that's all you're capable of. But I've got a new punch line for you. The Broomstick Missile is off the launching pad. The guidance-system plans are in a fat envelope heading for the CIA in Washington. You're too late, my friend.'

Questikian went slack-jawed and lost his sense of humor. I never expected him to fire that stubby Luger he carried, but he surprised both of us and pulled the trigger twice. The bullets slammed me back against the wall, but I bounced and hit him with my right hand and discovered I couldn't use my left. One blow was enough, however. His sparrow's body crumpled, and once I had him under my hands, I knew I owed the free world the favor of killing him. I went about the job with cold precision, putting my palm firmly over his mouth and pinching his nostrils with my fingers. He bucked a few times, like a dying fish, and then went speedily to hell.

By the time I was through, my left shoulder was beating like a bass drum in a mummers' parade. I staggered to my study and, with tears of pain in my eyes, peeled off my blood-soaked jacket. No, that was wrong, there wasn't a drop of blood on my coat or shirt. I fell into the chair behind the desk, pulled my notebook toward me and wrote:

Frank —

Writing this as effect of the drug recedes, but if past experience repeats, myosergicin will take over again in approximately 15 minutes. Unlike most hallucinogens, myosergicin seems to have total hallucinatory effect; no trace of reality left during periods of involvement. For God's sake, Frank, don't wait too long to find antidote; am convinced these hallucinations leading to stoppage of heart action. Not five minutes ago took two hallucinatory bullets in chest from hallucinatory agent of Smersh or something, and while I have not yet made reading, am certain blood pressure dangerously high. Anyway, facts. Took ten c.c.s of myosergicin – believe we should rename drug melodramine because of nature of hallucinations it inspires – on Saturday, April 4, 2:30 P.M. *After ten minutes, severe nose-bleed and headache warned me of extraordinary rise in blood pressure, receding quickly upon realization that I was armed. This part hard to explain. Found hallucinatory shoulder holster and service revolver on my person, and the realization that I had a weapon somehow succeeded in calming me down. Theory: Drug causes critical rise in pressure and melodramatic fantasy created by mind reduces pressure until action leads to crisis point (viz., the bullet wounds). Frank, if Questikian had aimed better, I'd be dead now. But there is no Questikian, is there? Getting confused. Melodramine – I mean myosergicin – must be taking over again. Why did I ever fool around with this damned stuff? Frank, if you can't work out antidote, I'm a dead man. See my notes on formulation, pages 83–95 of workbook. And for God's sake, don't move me; remember what happened to hamsters. General symptoms at present: weakness, sweating of palms, nervousness, headache, pounding, pounding. Someone at door; not sure if real or hallucinatory.*

Hal

'I trust you were expecting me.'

She swept into the room with an imperious flourish of her fur-fringed coat. I judged her to be a woman in her 30s, much too artful to let you determine her exact years. She held onto the jeweled handle of her umbrella as delicately as if it were a porcelain teacup. However, a certain coarseness about her hands led me to say:

'Tell me something, Lady Ortinby. Did you meet your husband in a restaurant or in his own kitchen?'

Dragons are said to emit fire from their mouths, but beautiful angry women flash it from their eyes.

'Sir! Who has told you about me?'

'Beyond the fact that you called for this appointment, I know nothing,' I said. 'However, I recognize that ailment common to kitchen employees which might be called scullery knuckles.'

She smiled grudgingly. 'Yes,' she said, 'I have heard you are clever. But it's not cleverness I need. It's nerve!'

'Ah.' I showed her to a chair.

'As you have so neatly determined,' Lady Ortinby expounded, 'I was a poor kitchenmaid when Lord Ortinby flattered me with his attentions, and when I became his bride two months ago, there wasn't a happier woman in England. However, my happiness was doomed to be short-lived because of – certain communications I fervently wish had never been written.'

'Love letters, Lady Ortinby?'

'Intimate letters,' she said, coloring to the roots of her exquisite coiffure, 'written with a passion long since spent. And some anonymous fiend has been using them to extort funds from me that I can ill afford to pay.'

'You did not think of the police?'

'My husband, sir, *is* the police!' And, of course, I recollected then that Lord Ortinby had recently been appointed deputy commissioner of the Yard.

'A difficult and delicate situation,' I said, 'but surely one best faced by honesty. A blackmailer's pockets can never be filled, my good woman. Why not make a clean breast of the affair?'

'I cannot!' she cried. 'My husband is insanely jealous, and I swore to him upon our betrothal that there had been no other loves before him. I cannot tell him the truth, nor can I continue to meet this blackmailer's exorbitant demands. There is only one solution: I must recover those damnable letters! Will you help me?'

'By what means?'

'I have never confronted my blackmailer in person; all my instructions have come by telephone. But I have refused to pay another penny unless he appears and shows me that he truly possesses these letters.'

'Good heavens!' I said. 'Have you been accepting him at his word?'

'No,' she said and fumbled within her purse. 'He has sent me one sample.' She thrust an envelope toward me. By its delicate weight and faint perfume I recognized its romantic errand. But, in addition to the address, I recognized still another marking on the envelope and caught my breath in surprise and sudden understanding.

'Lady Ortinby,' I began – but the sentence was to remain unfinished. The door of my flat burst open and almost fell from its hinges. The hulking figure of a man in a checkered greatcoat exploded into the room, brandishing a silver lion-headed stick as if he meant to use it as a weapon.

'Hubert!' Lady Ortinby cried. 'You followed me!'

'Yes!' he bellowed and seemed about to bring that club of a walking stick down upon her fragile white brow. 'So *this* is the ladyfriend you went to meet this afternoon!'

I stepped between them quickly.

'You misjudge your wife, Lord Ortinby; if she lied to you, it was only for fear of your displeasure. Her business with me is purely professional.'

'Professional!' he roared, going purple about the jowls. 'I'll give you professional business, you jackal! I'll have you locked up—'

'*You will do nothing of the kind!*'

The biting edge of my words brought him to his sanity, and his furor subsided.

'No, Lord Ortinby,' I said icily, 'you will not again misuse your office as deputy commissioner of the Yard; you have done damage enough.'

'Misuse my office?' he said hoarsely. 'Sir, how dare—'

'What do you mean?' she gasped.

'It's elementary, my dear woman. One glance at this envelope revealed the sickening truth of this matter. It bears a date stamp commonly employed by the clerks at Scotland Yard upon receipt of evidence. This letter, madam, came to you by way of the police.'

'But that's impossible!'

'Only too possible. Evidently the Yard apprehended a felon who had these letters in his possession. In the course of the investigation, they came to the desk of your husband; his maniacal jealousy drove him to torture you with them. Lady Ortinby, behold your blackmailer!'

'You *devil!*' Lord Ortinby roared. The lion-headed cane flashed in a silver arc, and I could not avoid the murderous blow that struck my collarbone and surely fractured it. I glimpsed the eyes of a man gone berserk as he lifted the stick again and brought it crashing down on my skull. Even as I lost consciousness, I knew that the madman would never be satisfied until he had bludgeoned every faint impulse of life from my body.

Saw the ceiling and knew that I was on the sofa. Both Lord and Lady Ortinby were gone. I tried to deduce what had occurred from the condition of the room. I found myself utterly incapable of making an intelligent surmise and then remembered that I was 100 percent New Jersey–born American and why the hell was I *thinking* with an English accent? I pushed myself into sitting position and discovered that an anvil had been sewn inside my skull. But I went to the desk and found my notebook, opened, thank God, and covered with Frank's cramped, unpunctuated, lovely scrawl.

Hal —

Arrived 9:20 and found you in study chair in what appeared to be coma Upon reading your notes tried to bring you around with injection meprobamate recalling its efficacy as antidote for other hallucinogens but results negative Hal this was crazy stunt you must have known danger of drug after hamsters death how could you be so stupid Have gone to lab to try and work out something If you can manage call me there

Frank

The fingers of my right hand felt like five lead cylinders, but I succeeded in dialing the number. It was some time before Frank answered, and I knew he must be absorbed with retorts and microscope. Then he spoke, but instead of the relief I expected to hear in his voice, there was anxiety and even hysteria.

'Hal!' he said. 'Thank God – I was hoping —' He made a gasping noise. 'Hal, you've got to get over here right away. The yellow fungus —'

'The what? Frank, what's going on there?'

'The fungus we scraped from the meteorite! Hal, it's spreading. Clinging – to everything! On my legs now – my arm – spreading —'

There was a clatter and a succession of meaningless – no, God help me, meaningful – sounds! Quiet, gentle Frank, who never raised his voice above a murmur, was screaming. Screaming!

I slammed the phone into its cradle and grabbed my coat. On an impulse, I found the bulky army automatic I had kept untouched in a bureau drawer and shoved the muzzle under my belt. Then I went out.

As I headed into the street, the shadow of the saucer which had been hovering over the city for the past 11 days made a pool of darkness that added to my gloom and the sense of impending disaster. Now it seemed odd to me that Frank and I had never connected the meteorite with that menacing shadow. When it appeared in the heavens, to instill unreasoning panic in the populace and start wild speculations about Russian attack and outer-space invasion, we had joined the scientific skeptics in the argument that it was only a meteorological phenomenon, some kind of atmospheric mirage. Telescopes had failed to penetrate its secret, and high-altitude planes had failed to reach it. Then the peculiar diamond-shaped meteorite had been discovered, and Frank was determined to probe its yellow fungus. Had he succeeded – only too well?

I hailed a taxi and snapped the address to the driver. We had gone only half a dozen blocks when he made an unexpected turn down a street darkened into the semblance of night by the saucer's shadow.

'Hey!' I said. 'This isn't the way to Fourth Street—'

'Mister, I—' He turned an agonized face toward me, his fingers white on the wheel. 'I can't help myself! I can't control this buggy!'

I heard the cabby's yowl as he tried to stop his plunging vehicle and I braced myself for a crash; I never anticipated the sensation that followed. *The taxi was leaving the ground.* It was being lifted into the air as if by a giant's fingers, and careless fingers at that. I was hurled against the side of the car as was the driver, but my door held and his didn't. I heard his shriek of terror as he clung to the door handle, but the giant that had us in its grip shook him loose into nothing and at the same time battered me into unconsciousness.

When I opened my eyes, I wished I hadn't. Before me was

a floating balloon of flesh that made my gorge rise and almost unhinged my sanity. It swayed hypnotically, its single red-veined orb fixing me with an unblinking, lidless stare, the stringy, liver-colored appendages dangling from the thing, swaying as if in a breeze. I turned my head away from the sight and glimpsed a gleaming complexity of machinery; I tried to move and realized that I was imprisoned by a 'chair' of some spongy substance that left only my hands free. Without reasoning, I knew where I was and what I faced. I was inside the space ship that was darkening the earth, and I was confronting the spokesman of the alien race which had brought it there.

'Speak,' said a voice inside my head. 'I will understand you. I am Jushru the Overseer. Your mind is filled with questions, and it is my will to answer.'

'My friend!' I gasped, somehow certain that this creature would know Frank's fate. 'What has become of him?'

'The Flikkari has covered him,' said the voice, 'as the Flikkari will soon cover all. Our estimate is two lunar periods. I anticipate your next question. What is the Flikkari?'

'Yes,' I said, trying not to think, not of Frank, not of earth, not of anything.

'The Flikkari is an enzyme,' Jushru the Overseer said. 'It is the detergent with which we shall scour and cleanse your planet of its undesirable life and foliation. When the process is completed to our standards, we will bring our vessels and our people to your planet. Thus do we populate the galaxies. We are the Stushuri, inheritors of the universe.'

'And I?'

'For my collection,' Jushru said delicately. 'You are a prize specimen, you know. In all my travels through the cosmos I have never met your physiological equal, with your loose skin flapping about and the strange metallic appendage on your hip. . . .'

I realized then that Jushru, for all his intelligence, had not yet recognized that my 'skin' was clothing and that the metal appendage was my army automatic. The knowledge that my weapon was still with me filled me with sudden hope – not that I could be saved, but that at least the Overseer of the Stushuri might die with me. Carefully, I took the gun into my hand and pointed it at the thing that bobbed before me.

'Would you like to know the purpose of the appendage?' I asked.

'Yes, specimen,' Jushru replied heartily, and I fired. The bullet hit the balloon of flesh and it splattered with an ugly sound. Splattered, exploded and was no more, and simultaneously, deprived of its captain, the ship gave a sickening lurch and started to descend. If the spongy arms of the chair hadn't held me, I would have been dashed to pieces against the bulkhead of the vessel, but I knew it would not be long before mother earth herself would welcome me in thunder and death, and I prayed that my act hadn't come too late to save the human race. . . .

Raised myself from the soft ground and looked about for signs of wreckage. There wasn't a thing on the carpet. Could I have crashed through the roof of my own apartment house? I shook my head to rid it of this ludicrous notion and stumbled to the desk, hoping that there would be further word from the laboratory. There was.

Hal —

Found your notes and have developed antidote along lines you suggested. Will return as soon as experiments on lab animals completed Hal am gravely concerned whether antidote merely intensifies or alters nature of myosergicin's effects but if animals survive tests will return within few hours and make the attempt

Frank

My nose was bleeding. I knew it was the result of my heightened blood pressure, and I quickly pressed my handkerchief to my face. I didn't like the way the count was staring at me across the room. 'Perhaps it's the altitude,' I said gaily.

'Your mountainous country doesn't suit a lowlander like myself, Count.'

His lips parted in a smile, and once again I remarked his unusual long white canines with their gleaming points. I refused to give credence to the superstitious tales of the villagers, and yet. . . .

'Your blood is very red,' the count said with a disarming chuckle. 'It is a shame to lose so much of it for a mere nose-bleed.'

'And just how,' said the Oriental leaning against the carved mantelpiece, 'do you suggest blood should be lost, Count? In what service besides bestial appetite?'

The count snarled audibly at this, but the Oriental, tugging at his long mustache, merely smiled. His other hand lightly stroked the dark hair of the lovely sloe-eyed woman who sat beside him, and I cringed at the sight of his talonlike nails on her white skin. I knew, of course, how determined he was to eradicate the Caucasian race in its entirety and I wouldn't have been surprised to see that hand signal to his dacoits to garrot the lot of us. Mata, however, seemed fearless.

'There is only one honorable way to shed one's blood,' she said coolly, 'and that, of course, is in the service of one's country. Don't you agree with that, *Monsieur* Egypt?'

I followed her eyes to the pudgy little man on the sofa. He wore a red fez and appeared to be asleep, and I realized with a start how closely he resembled the late Peter Lorre. I was almost ready to comment on the resemblance when Bogart entered the room brandishing the hand grenade. I tried to tell him whose side I was on, but when I glanced down and saw the Nazi uniform I wore, I was no longer certain myself. In the distance I could hear the pounding of Japanese cannon and the ugly buzz of the Zeros overhead. When the tear-gas bomb exploded in the room, I tried to find my way to the cupboard where the artillery was stored, but that dirty fink Nitti had hidden the key and all I could find was one stinking tommy gun. I spit out all its bullets at the cops in the street until they blinded me with their spotlight. I had to get out of there, because I knew Maria would be waiting for me on the bridge, and I had promised to bring the dynamite before nightfall. The roof was my only avenue of escape, and I would have gained my freedom easily if that damned music-hall mentalist hadn't reached it before me and brought a hundred Viennese policemen into the chase. Luckily, I caught a dangling vine and swung over the precipice to the next cliff, but found myself surrounded by a pack of lions intent upon making me their midday meal. I cried out to Simba, and my old friend responded and led them away. It wasn't hard to pick up the trail of Denham and the rest; all I had to do was listen for their cries of terror as they fled from the path of Kong. Suddenly my foot became entangled with a monstrous root and I went crashing to the jungle floor, my ankle twisting underneath me. Crippled, I watched the fearsome Brontosaurus lumber toward me, and even the sight of my rescuers didn't succeed in calming my fears, for I recognized their ragged uniforms and the tricolor sashes at their waists and wondered what kind of death I would make at the foot of the guillotine; but no, even that quick end was to be denied me, for when I looked up and saw the blade, it was swinging, swinging like a gigantic pendulum, drawing ever closer, closer, until finally its razor-sharp edge slit through my clothing and I could bear the suspense no longer and opted for the Pit....

Climbed out and of course saw that my shirt was gone, no doubt slashed to pieces. There was, however, a strip of adhesive on my left biceps. I lifted myself from the study chair and found myself too weak to move. It was an effort even to bring the notebook in front of my eyes. There was a thin scrawl from Frank, but my vision was so blurred by whatever substance he had injected into my blood stream that it took me a full five minutes to decipher the message.

Hal—

The lab animals responded positively to the antidote

but am still not sure of its efficacy However feel obliged to try as myosergicin seems to be having increased deleterious effect on your system Gave you 20 c.c.s Will return shortly Pray this is the answer

Frank

When I heard the knock at the door, I knew at once that Frank wasn't my middle-of-the-night caller. Frank owned a rude set of knuckles, and this was a gentle tapping, so discreet that I knew a woman would respond to my 'Come in!'

It was indeed a woman, the beautiful Lady Isobel whose husband, Lord Drago, ruled this principality with an iron hand. Evidently that hand was lacking in human warmth; with white bosom heaving, Lady Isobel pulled me into her boudoir and locked the door. I laughed as I unbuckled my sword and said, 'Ods blood, milady, this is a turn for the better! When I arrived with the queen's party, you seemed disdainful of a mere member of the royal escorts.'

'Your reputation had preceded you,' she said coyly, 'and I could do nothing to make my husband suspicious.'

'And now?'

'And now,' the lady said, 'with His Lordship safely in consultation with the queen's deputies, you may proceed to live up to that reputation.'

Live up to it I did and would have perhaps exceeded her expectations if Lord Drago had not thoughtlessly returned from his conference and entered the bedroom. With an oath, he lunged at me with his sword and, having time for neither dressing nor defending, I wisely chose the open window and the trailing ladders of ivy. 'Guards! Guards!' he shouted, and the clatter of their boots sounded all about me. Fortunately, a helping hand, belonging to a shapely ladies' maid named Françoise, came to my rescue.

'In here!' she whispered, showing me into her darkened bedchamber. I breathed a sigh of relief, which she plainly interpreted as one of passion. She flung herself into my arms, and I soon learned that her lowly station diminished neither her charms nor her ardor. Yet even as we sported I sensed an alien presence in the room and lifted myself from her arms to see the glowering face of a young serving-man who held a candle aloft that cast moving shadows of our dalliance on the wall.

'Rudolpho!' she screamed. 'My husband!'

Rudolpho's oath was earthier than His Lordship's, and his weapon was a wicked knife which he drew from his shirt-waist. I met his attack with an upraised pillow, but knowing I would be no match for his brawn in my weakened state, made my escape through fleetness of foot. By this time, the alarum was general throughout the palace and, out-numbered, unarmed and undressed, I chuckled at the turning of fate that had brought me to this pass, and when I heard the up-stairs door creak open and saw the queen herself beckon me toward her, I vaulted the stairs and prepared once more to do battle in the name of liberty, equality and fraternity.

As the sun came up, the golden peak of the minaret flashed into my eyes and I sat up quickly, remembering to praise Allah that I had lived to see another dawn. I gathered my rags about me and prepared to venture forth once more into the crowded streets of Baghdad, in the hope that some nobleman would pity my hunger. The morning was almost gone when I saw eunuchs with staves marching before the harem of some great sultan, and as I moved my worthless self from their path I heard a woman's voice cry:

'Seize him! Seize that beggar!'

And, lo, the eunuchs placed their hands upon me and bound me with ropes and, despite my cries, bore me to the magnificence of the sultan's palace. I trembled with fear for my young life, even as the slave girls stripped me of my rags, scrubbed and cleansed and perfumed me with rose water and gave me the splendid clothes of a prince to wear. I was then brought into a great hall where singing women beat upon taborets and dancing women undulated their bodies like flowers, the petals of their clothing offering tantalizing

glimpses of their naked loveliness; and seated upon the cushions, drawing my eyes like the rising of the full moon, was a beautiful lady of the sultan's harem. She held out her jeweled hand and spoke:

'Welcome, welcome, O mighty one,' she said. 'Welcome to us, Chosen of Allah.'

I fell upon my knees and begged for explanation and heard these words:

'Mighty one, thou art the lost son of the Sultan Haroun-el-Akbar, stolen from your inheritance by a wicked sorcerer. But now we have found you again, and all the wonders of your domain and your palace are yours again, for – alas! – your father, the Sultan Haroun-el-Akbar, is dead. For thirty moons we have been without our beloved lord and have yearned for the day when we might find his son, our master.'

And thus saying, the beautiful woman drew me toward her, and I knew delights such as no mortal man, Haroun-el-Akbar excepted, had ever known. And even as the long night ended, I knew that she was only one of the harem's many treasures and that I was the most blessed of men. Not because I was the son of a sultan – for, indeed, I was only the son of Abu Kir, a lowly dealer in carpets – but because Allah, in his compassion, had placed me in a harem that had grown tired of waiting....

Once again the sun was in my eyes, but I opened them and saw Scarlett at the vanity, plaiting her auburn hair, and I chuckled and pulled at her dressing gown, and while she made soft, cooing southern sounds of protest, she let the silken robe slip and slide down over her shoulders and across her legs, and I picked her up in my arms and carried her up the winding stairway. By the time I was ready to come downstairs again, the party was in full sway, the drums pounding and the strings throbbing, and I tightened the sash about my waist, lit a cigarette and snapped my finger on the brim of my hat before moving out onto the dance floor where Carlotta gyrated sensuously to the rhythm of the tango. At my touch she shivered and then yielded to me as a partner of the dance, and her eyes promised that later she would be my partner in love.... But other eyes were seeking mine – the *contessa*, stripping off her clothes in the middle of a bored circle of spectators, a sight that the damned photographers of Rome would have given their eyeteeth to witness. Very well, I thought wearily, I will make the *vita* a little more *dolce* for you, *Contessa*, and nodded my head. She ran toward me eagerly, but I snarled and stuck the cold muzzle of the .38 against her soft white belly and then kissed her hard on the mouth. Her kiss was like candy. 'Goodness gracious,' she said, 'I'm only a little girl child, and I don't think daddy would like this at all.' I didn't care what her daddy-o thought, man. I mean, like, I didn't give a damn. I mean, like, her and me, we had this date a long time, and even if dames were like streetcars, tonight was the night, dig? And so I ordered the Nubians to depart and drew the curtains, and slowly removed the splendor of her garments, except for the Egyptian crown that topped her imperious queenly head. 'Are you really Playmate of the Year?' I whispered. 'Call me Sophia,' she said and held me close. When she finally let me go, I made my way to the study desk and wrote:

Frank —

Stuff you gave me no antidote at all, merely changed hallucinatory point of view. For God's sake, keep a record of the formula; it's worth a million bucks. And don't worry about finding antidote. If this damned stuff is going to kill me, it's not a bad way to die.

Hal

My Head's in a Different Place, Now

GRANIA DAVIS

LIVING ON welfare is one of the biggest bummers in the whole world. To apply, you stand for hours in some huge long line, your kid in your arms, all fussy and wet. When you finally get seen, some bitchy clerk tells you that you filled out line 67 in the forms wrong, and you have to redo the whole thing and go back to the end of the line.

If you're sick, you crawl on the bus to this clinic, and hope there'll be a seat for you in the hot airless waiting room, cause you know it'll be maybe three, four hours. They tell everyone to get there at eight, and send you home if you're late, but the doctors don't show up till maybe 9:30, and by the time it's your turn it's maybe eleven or (twelve is lunch for the doctors) one o'clock ... and your kid is in your lap, screaming and drooling. (No bread for baby-sitters, man.)

And if you're too sick to make it to the bus, but not sick enough for an ambulance, like maybe you sprained your ankle and can't walk to the bus stop, well then, tuff titty, sister, you don't see any doctor at all, and you end up with a bum ankle for the rest of your life.

And you can't get into a decent apartment, cause even if you could afford the rent, they won't rent to welfare freaks, so you end up in some raunchy flop-house, overlooking an airshaft, where the roaches are running across your kid's face at night and eating holes in your dirty clothes to get out the little bits of food.

The fascist papers make it sound like welfare's some kind of groovy trip and like everyone is lying and cheating to rip-off the taxpayers' bread ... but, like, what the hell would you do if you had this two-year-old kid, and the day-care centers had a waiting list two miles long ... and if you had no high-school diploma or job-training of any kind? You can get a job sometimes scrubbing floors, but nothing that'd support both you and your kid, *and* a full-time baby-sitter.

I was kinda thinking to put my kid in Head-Start when she's a little older ... and maybe take a class in something so I could get a part-time job ... somewhere ... if I could find one....

My old man's on welfare, too. He keeps psyching out. He's into a big intellectual and revolutionary bag, an anarchist, but figures he might as well make use of the government until it can be destroyed. He's a Leo, with Taurus rising.

People are always saying to him, 'Wow, the freedom part sounds really fine, but wouldn't people get on a heavy violence trip and start runnin' around, doing each other in?'

His eyes get all big, and his red-bearded face starts to twitch with excitement as he explains, 'People are *already* running around, doin' each other in. Haven't you heard of "crime in the streets"? And the government, with all its wars, has done in more people than 10,000 Jack-the-Rippers ever could. The government doesn't give a damn about protecting you and me, it only protects the rich and the powerful, because that's all it cares about, *power*, power over us with the pigs, power over other governments with missiles and bombs ... power for the rich to get richer, power for the oil companies to pollute our water, power for the auto-makers to make uselessly huge, fast cars that run around, doin' people in. But if people had a sense of individual freedom and dignity, and could do their own thing, then a lot of hate and anger would disappear.'

It's a heavy trip, being an anarchist, and every now and then it just gets too heavy for him and he, like, just ... freaks out ... and has to take a little trip to the loony bin. They dope him up, and calm him down, and then he's all right, for a while.

It's kinda hard, never being sure if his head's gonna be together, from one day to the next, but we really have a lot of telepathy, both in and out of bed ... and he hasn't been bugging out, too much ... lately....

The only thing that made welfare at all groovy was our social worker, Phil, a truly righteous dude ... truly. Not only did he turn us on whenever we came in for an interview (he always kept a few joints stashed around in his office), and lay extra bus tickets and food stamps on us, but it was him that passed on the word about the new ruling that if the social worker was willing to do the paper work, you could leave the city, or even the country, and still get your check.

Good news, man. First we thought of going on up to Oregon, and starting a little farm in the woods. But then we decided that this whole *country* is so uptight and fascist, with only plastic, expensive shit in the stores, and the air and water slowly poisoning us to death ... and eventually Moonbeam (that's my daughter, a Gemini and a truly tender little joy-freak) would be forced into one of their concentration camp schools, where they'd fuck her head, just like they did ours.

So we finally decided to split, entirely, and go off to Mexico to groove with the cheap prices and the warm sun and the Indians, who are a bunch of truly righteous heads, all the time bombed out on peyote and grass and magic mushrooms, and everyone's relaxed and smiling and, like, together.

But we'd also been reading in the *Tribe* how some of the Mexican police have been really hassling hairs, and then, neither one of us spoke Spanish, let alone *Aztec*, or whatever the Indians speak ... but if karma is building you up for something, it's gonna come. So one night this dude, a Maoist, who my old man used to know, showed up looking for a place to crash, and he tells us about how a friend of his has just come back from a tropical island, a *paradise*, man, right off the coast of Central America, but *English* speaking, cause it was once owned by England, who sent runaway slaves there as a punishment.

But these slaves really got it together and mixed with the Indians, and started little farms and built little villages, and fished and hunted and sang and danced, and shared everything they owned with anyone who needed it. And you can go down there and just sit on the beach, and get stoned, man, and pick coconuts off the trees, and everyone's friendly and free, no bad vibes. You can rent a little hut for practically nothing, no plastic tourist shit, and everything is really organic and together with the earth.

Wow! We got high just hearing about it . . . and the *I Ching* said 'It furthers one to cross the great water.' So, like what further proof did we need that we had truly found *the* place?

The trip down was beautiful. We hitched along the coast, past the huge cliffs covered with redwoods and Monterey cypress. Wow, the yellow sage smelled so sweet, and the water swirling around the rocks below was all mescaline colored . . . blue, green, red. . . .

Brothers and Sisters in vans and campers gave us rides, fed us, turned us on . . . past the curving beige hills . . . through the L.A. and San Diego tracts ('Acne on an adolescent landscape,' said my old man) . . . surfing bums, beach houses. . . . Then things starting to look a little seamy and Mexican as we neared the border.

Fortunately, no hassle with the border guards, who weren't expecting us to smuggle grass *into* Mexico! Tijuana . . . a million places advertising MARRIAGE/DIVORCE. 'Shit,' says my old man, 'if we believed in legal bondage, we could get married and divorced in one day . . . or vice versa.' Nightclubs, cheap Mexican schlock at high gringo prices, but you could smell the tortillas and the piss, so you *knew* you were in Mexico.

We went to the Three Stars bus station and waited around for a second class bus to Mexico City. When it arrived we grabbed the roomy back seat, where Moonbeam could move a little, and turning on, we settled back to groove with the desert, and the peddlers selling hot potato tacos for 3c each, and the buzzards ... and people getting on and off, little old ladies in shawls with huge bundles ... and the bus broke down, lots, and all the men would pile out and look at the engine and jabber excitedly in Spanish, then they'd make everyone (including the old ladies) get out and help push. But we dug it; we aren't on a heavy time trip like most gringos.

Mexico City smelled like exhaust fumes and wood smoke. Big old churches sinking and tilting in the soft sand, Indian ladies with black-haired babies squatting nearby, selling squash seeds in neat little piles. Traffic. Noise. All day and night, lots of strong vibes, but not much hate. Big glasses of fresh, natural orange juice for 8c. We've all got the shits now, but figure we'll build up an immunity to it like the Indians. I tell my old man I'm all out of diapers. He says, 'Oh, just let her crap in the street, what's more organic than shit?' His head is in a really wise place when he isn't freaking out.

Another bus down to Yucatan, out of the desert-mountain country, into the jungle ... a total gas ... all the greens, I've always dug green. Tangled green vines, sluggish green rivers, and birds. Big white ones with long necks. 'Egrets,' says my old man.

People are living in round thatched huts and old box-cars all decorated with birdcages and flowers. Naked babies and pigs are rooting around. Peddlers are selling us pineapples, and we're sweating and shitting, man, shitting and sweating....

We expected Merida to be some primitive jungle town, so our minds were slightly blown by the big fancy buildings, the tile and stained glass, and the marble love seats in the plaza, over which huge flocks of crows flew at sunset. 'Right on the nineteenth century trade routes,' explained my old man. 'Bourgeois capitalist pigs.'

But despite the European look, there were crowds of Mayan Indians in far-out, embroidered shifts, and you could take a bus to visit ruined pyramids, all jungly and overgrown like out of a cheapy adventure flick ... and my old man got on this trip like we were in all kinds of camp movies and books that had been laid in his brain when he was in college and still into that kind of artificial head shit. He starts rapping like what if Tarzan came swinging on that big vine, or maybe we'll find Mighty Joe Young behind that tree, peacefully chewing on a banana....

We farted around in Yucatan until it was time for our weekly 'coastal-and-inter-island ferry' to leave. 'Pure Joseph Conrad,' sighed my old man. 'The wine dark sea ...' Mostly a cargo boat, with benches for the passengers to sit on and a canvas awning to protect you from the sun and rain. Indians ... blacks ... a few Chinese and Eurasian businessmen ... a couple of Australians going around the world in shorts ... and some beautiful people that were a mixture of everything. Babies ... lunches in earthen pots ... animals with their legs tied together ... bales, crates, bundles.

We lucked out with a psychedelic red and purple sunset ... shared some of our grass ... shared their rotgut aguardiente and thick tortillas with black beans and chilis. Then we hit a rain squall, wind. The canvas was about as useful as a torn rubber, but we didn't let it bring us down, just grooved with it, while Moonbeam curled up on a blanket, asleep with a bunch of other kids like puppies. Stopped all through the night at little ports ... the boat rocked and swayed, but no sweat, cause everyone knows that grass is good for seasickness. Around noon the next day we finally got to where we were going ... the paradise, man, Jobo's Caye.

The water was too shallow for the boat to sail in, so dugouts sail out to load and unload cargo and passengers. We climbed down the ladder with an old black woman and several chickens, and urged Moonbeam to jump into our arms.

The black boatman gave us a big smile and started rowing to the shore where we could see little white-washed wooden houses, on stilts with tin roofs glinting, and lots of palm trees. A few people in thin, nondescript clothes, the men carrying machetes, were meeting the boats and singing a little chanting song. A real upper, and we offer the boatman some grass. His smile gets even bigger.

Man, like this is really *it!* 'Hey,' says my old man, 'we're Bob Hope and Bing Crosby starring in *The Road to Jobo's Caye*. We're making slightly dirty remarks (but only *slightly*) about all the sexy women and pretty soon Dorothy Lamour is going to show up with a sarong and *adventures!*'

The capital, Bender Creek Town, was a backwater little place. Houses and shacks, puddles in the main street, in which ducks were swimming. Public water faucets and outhouses every few blocks. A few Chinese-owned stores, a few Land-Rovers ... old black women selling fruit, parrots and fried conch in the market ... a government building on a small square ... a fly-filled, shuttered room in a rickety hotel. The vibes were good, but it was hot, crowded and polluted.

The people were really welcoming to strangers, and would come right up to rap with us on the street. A lot of them were trying to get sponsors to come to America and make the affluence scene. My old man tried to tell them to forget that shit. In America they'd be hated and spat at. They'd have no freedom and no dignity. But they just smiled slow smiles and we could tell that their heads were into plumbing and refrigerators and cars and all the plastic crap we were trying to get away from.

We decided we wanted to go into one of the bush villages where it was *really* different, where the people were really into the here and now and there were no government buildings and stores and that kind of Americanized shit.

One dude we're rapping with on the waterfront starts telling us about this village he was raised in. On a little peninsula, surrounded by a big lagoon ... Sea Dog Bank ... there were so many mangoes they were used to feed the pigs. Everyone sat in the sun, grooving together, sharing, singing and digging each day. Wow! it really sounded like *the* place, a paradise!

The little ferry that went there, twice a month, was leaving in a few days, and when it left we were on board with the boatman, a few packages and bundles, and two drunk young brothers holding an enormous bin of cucumbers.

We started up slimy, green Bender Creek, and soon found ourselves in a shallow, twisty canal through a thick mangrove swamp. Birds we couldn't see were screeching, fish we couldn't see were splashing, insects we couldn't see were biting us, and once we heard a loud 'plop' and saw a small, grayish crocodile swimming alongside the boat.

'Moonbeam, get your hands out of the water, baby!' Wow, I hate to restrict her freedom like that, but there aren't even any clinics around here!

The air was like a warm, wet washcloth and my old man was into a heavy number about how this was the *African Queen*, and he was Humphrey Bogart and I was Katharine Hepburn and we were being chased by Germans and blood sucking leeches. No loony bins around here, either....

'The Garden of Eden,' is what my old man started calling Sea Dog Bank, 'from the oldest, campest book of all.'

And it really was a together spot. Our friend at Bender Creek Town had told us that there wasn't much use for bread there, but if we stocked up on some presents we would get right into the good vibes of the place ... so (on his advice) we bought some cloth, honey, cheap flashlights, rum and canned stuff and (my old man feeling like Columbus) started laying it on the brothers and sisters who came to meet the boat. Well, it like really freaked them out and they started hugging us and welcoming us, without even knowing our *names*. Wow, their heads were in such a *giving* place.

The big, boss Mamma of the place, Miz Rose, finally shows up, and hearing that we aren't planning to go back with the ferry, but are actually thinking to *live* here, she gets the most turned-on look on her face and starts ordering her daughters around in a shrill jabber that we later found out was a mixture of African, Carib Indian and English picked up from wandering ministers and a few transistor radios. 'The Tower of Babel,' mumbles my old man. I really don't know what he's talking about half the time, but he's been doing a lot less of that, lately.

Miz Rose must've had about a million daughters, all by her shriveled little one-legged husband who hunted crocodiles and had once had to cut off his own leg with a machete when it was bitten by a poisonous snake out in the bush. Before we could even finish a joint, the daughters had led us to this neat, funky little hut whose owner had recently died. It had dirt floors and a thatch roof (full of all kinds of creepy-crawly things, but harmless and beautiful . . . not like city bugs which reflect everyone's hate vibes). There was a straw mattress on a wooden frame, a cooking hearth, a few candles, and tin dishes, and not much else. . . . Zen as all hell. We were told that we could crash here for $5 a month.

One of the daughters, pretty, but almost toothless, demanded all our dirty clothes and, laughing like I was a little kid when I offered to help, marched off with the bundle on her head to scrub them in the pond. Another daughter brought us a bucket of natural rain-water from the big wooden vat in which it's collected and stored. Another one brought us a basket of fruit, and Miz Rose herself, all 250 pounds of her, jabbering orders to everyone she passed, brought us a big armadillo shell in which pieces of armadillo (tastes like chicken), fish, breadfruit, and plantain had been steamed in coconut milk.

Outa sight! A *paradise!* In front of our hut were coconut palms and an immense mango tree with orchids crawling up the trunk. A little white beach led to the front lagoon where people swam and the men fished. Behind the huts were the gardens, chickens and pigs, which the women tended, and eventually, the back lagoon where the outhouses were, with hungry, shit-eating catfishes swimming underneath, and where *nobody* swam or fished.

There was no garbage dump. What the people didn't eat, the dogs and chickens ate . . . what they left the pigs ate. Anything that couldn't be eaten was burned for fuel or reused in some way. A total, organic ecology trip . . . and Moonbeam could wander naked, up and down the village, playing and bumming food, with no cars or any other danger to rip her off.

Wow, we were totally into grooving with the whole scene, for a while. Of course, it was hot, bitching hot, and we couldn't swim too far out into the lagoon, because of the sharks, or sit too long in the shallower water, because of the sun ... and the mosquitoes and sand fleas were into a heavy hostility trip ... and in the day, it was too hot to do much more than paddle in the lagoon or sit around getting stoned. In the night it was mostly too hot to sleep, but there was nothing else to do, so we slept anyway, with roosters crowing up and down the village at daybreak to let us know when the hour or so of coolish dawn had arrived and we could move around a little. We had read all our books and most of the cheap paperbacks which the boatman had bought for us in Bender Creek Town. (For a few bucks a month, he would pick up our check, mail any dope and any store shit we wanted for ourselves, or as presents for Miz Rose and her many daughters.) And, like there was nothing much we wanted to do, and nothing much we *had* to do, thanks to Miz Rose ... and, well, after a while our energy started getting low, really low. We were kind of thinking of going to a place we heard about up in the hills, where it was cooler, and really beautiful, with pine trees, and all ... a paradise ... but it was kind of hard to get from here to there.

One dawn morning, Miz Rose and her old man (who makes it better on one leg than most men would on three) stuck their heads into our curtained doorway and told us that the land crabs were running out in the bush, and would we like to go get us some.

We got dressed and came out. It seemed like everyone 'from six to sixty' as they say in the ads, was there with big burlap bags and long wooden tongs for picking up the crabs, and singing a little number about 'crab soup.' We left Moonbeam with one of the old folks and, for the first time, walked the mile or so to where the end of the village joins the low, bushy jungle.

There was a funky little tumbledown hut a little ways into the bush. It was leaning to one side, with mangy, sagging thatch. A sound of faint drumming came from inside, which was really a turn-on. We stopped in front of it, and Miz Rose boomed out, louder than ever, 'Brother Jo, bring us something against de do-do-mon!'

The drumming continued. 'He hearing good no more,' explained Miz Rose as she sent in one of her daughters who, after a bit, came out leading what must've been the oldest man I have ever seen. He was stiff, mostly blind with cataracts and half-deaf, but you could tell from the smile on his face that his head was in a truly beautiful and spiritual place.

'You get de lan' crab, eh?' he said in a high, cracked voice. 'Mind de do-do-mon don' snatch de li' ones!'

Miz Rose walked up and yelled directly into his ear, 'Give us something against de do-do-mon!'

'Eh?'

'Something against de do-do-mon!' she bellowed.

He nodded and his smile got even broader. He began fumbling with some leather bags that hung around his neck. Finally he selected one and handed it to Miz Rose saying, 'You bring me some crab *soup*, hear?'

Miz Rose assured him we would, as he tottered back in to begin drumming and singing some more. Then she began to take tiny pieces of what looked like bark out of the little bag and feed them to everyone.

Whatever it was, it was a truly righteous gas. It had a very strong, sweet odor and we felt the flash immediately, like a joyful pop inside our heads. Then we were off on the clearest non-jittery, non-paranoid speed trip, which made cocaine seem like 7-up, but we knew it was something totally different, cause we could still smell the strong, sweet smell of it on our bodies.

'Right-on, brother Methuselah,' grooved my old man. 'You do deal in truly telepathic shit.'

We skipped off, giggling and talking with the rest, the men slashing the undergrowth with machetes, until we came to the crab holes. The crabs were big and blue with angry eyestalks and large, pinching claws. We couldn't manage to catch a single one . . . but everyone else soon had a big, writhing sackful, and we knew there'd be no shortage of crab soup in the village that night. Besides, the main idea in our heads was to pay a little visit to Brother Jo, to dig some of his drumming and to trip out on some more of his outasight, mind-bending herbs.

We mentioned this to Miz Rose on the way back and she told us that he was the bush healer, but very poor, and that he could tell us all kinds of far-out stories about the earliest people on Sea Dog Bank, and about some of the strange creatures that lived in the water and the bush. He could give you a song or a medicine for anything that was bugging you, and she was sure that if we brought a little present, he'd really dig to rap with us.

So the next morning we set off to his hut with some canned goods and a spare daughter to help us communicate.

It was almost completely dark inside, sour smelling and stifling, even in the early morning, with all kinds of creepy/crawly/biting things. There was a heap of sleeping straw and leaves in the corner, a lot of moldering food scraps, some wooden and deer-hide drums and some little piles of mushrooms, herbs, bark and other organic-looking goodies. 'Nothing plastic and bourgeois here,' my old man murmured.

It wasn't all that easy to rap with him, but he did a little joy number when we laid the canned goods on him, and gave us a great big smile when our guide-daughter blasted into his ear (in a voice that would have made her mother proud) an order to tell us some songs and stories!

He started off in an endless mixture of Spanish, African and Bible English to sing and mumble and croon and chuckle and preach . . . and like we could only dig about a third of what he was saying, and a lot of that was old-timey Christian cat-crap, but we sat there well into the afternoon, sweating and scratching, and, when the guide-daughter wasn't looking, sampling some of the herbs and getting high, and getting sleepy, and getting the farts, and feeling our heads getting lighter and purer . . . and every now and then our heads would get into the same space-time as his, and we'd start really tripping out on some story or song.

'De Ashi-pampi, dey li' people. Dey come at night an' dey eat de embers from de fire-hot, but dey no harm people.... An' dis song it cure de boils ... An' de Jack-O' Lantern, it be a big boat with many lantern. It sail into de lagoon on dark nights, but when de men go out for search in de dories, it disappear.... An' dis song I hear on de docks in de war ... *Run, Kaiser William, run for your life, for if the Russians get you, they'll surely take your wife....* An' dis root make a tea for quiet you liver.... An' de do-do-mon, him all cover wi' fur and he eyes be big and green an' he feet be webbed like a duck an' he live under de bushes. Sometime him sneak into de village at night and steal de baby who have lost de parents or de wife who have lost de husband. If you eat what de do-do-mon give you, you never come back, but if you no eat den de do-do-mon him let you go.... Dese mushroom is what de do-do-mon favor to eat, but it be poison for regular mon....'

The old brother pulled a few tiny, blackish dried mushrooms out of one of the little leather stash bags around his neck and showed them to us ... they looked pretty wicked in the dim, fly-buzzing light. As he put them away one of them dropped to the floor, and my old man and me looked at each other and grinned. We knew all about those 'poison' mushrooms, they usually contained the most turned-on shit ... and one certainly couldn't hurt, not shared between two people ... just a little 'recreational dose,' dig?

So my old man picked up the mushroom and we began to nibble on it, nice and slow, getting together with the woodsy taste....

And the old man was droning on. 'An' de greazy mon, him crawl in de window at night and molest de woman.... An' dis prayer to de Holy Mother, it be good for de toothache ...' And the mosquitoes were biting something fierce ... and it was hot ... and the guide-daughter was flaked out with her mouth open, snoring slightly ... and it was dark, *too dark*, we had to get into the *light* ... we yelled something about having to use the shithouse on the back lagoon and ran out of the hut.

Which way? Back to the village? No, too many people there ... might run into some rip-off vibes ... could already tell from the feeling in our stomachs that this was going to be a heavy trip. Into the bush, then, no one there ... can just groove with the trees.

So we darted up the path along the first growth of bush grasses and tangled trees and vines, and noticed that these mushrooms grew there quite commonly ... no trouble scoring if we want some more ... and then our heads like, well just *exploded*, I mean we were in a completely different *place!*

Everything was green, man, I mean like layer upon layer of swaying *green*. You couldn't see a tree or a leaf, just green ... prisms of green ... green that was yellow ... green that was blue or purple, or red ... and all kinds of strange creatures were floating around in the green.

A large frog and an egret were practicing karate chops on each other and then started hugging and kissing and going down on each other in the green. A large, bearded cockroach dressed like an elegant European movie-star strolled by and advised everyone to take the 21 day, thermal cure at Vichy. A tiny yellow female creature in a bathing suit bounced by, chanting *Om* and masturbating with a credit card in the green ... a flat flounder floated by with an enormous tray of far-out, gourmet food ... and a duck and a cow read Japanese fairy-tales ... in the green, the green, the prisms of green....

It must've taken several hours for us to come down ... though it could've taken several years, the way our time-sense was blown. Our heads felt pretty spaced, and our eyes were hugely dilated. Everything still looked kind of greenish and our tongues and skin had that kind of fuzzy feeling like after too much rot-gut, dago-red wine ... but you kind of expect that after a really mind-bending trip. We wandered back to the hut to explain to Brother Jo and the guide-daughter that we had done a little walk thing, and had gotten lost.

'You mind de snakes and de do-do-mon,' scolded the

daughter, and we let her shepherd us back to our hut and a big dinner of Miz Rose's iguana-tail soup (which tastes like chicken). We were pretty wasted and let Moonbeam curl up with some of Miz Rose's grandchildren, at her place, while we zonked out in our little hut.

The next day was boat-day, and we lay around, feeling kind of strung-out, till after lunch when everyone went down to the little wooden pier to wait for the monthly boat from 'de Big Town.'

Our packages, this month, had mostly chocolate bars, aspirin tabs and cigarettes, which everyone really dug. And the mail ... some of my old man's underground papers, a letter from my mother, and a formal looking letter from the welfare folks.

We ripped that one open right away, and it ripped *us* off right away, because it was a notice informing us that our social worker, Phil, had been busted (he must've gotten paranoid and the pigs could feel his vibes) and that our new social worker had 'too heavy a case-load to be able to do the intricate paper work involved in out-of-county payments.' And, if we didn't get our asses back to the City and County of San Francisco by *next month*, we'd be out of luck, welfare-wise. Shit ... or as they say in the comics ... #$%=&'(!!

I mean like, living here was cheap, but not *free*, for Christ sake, we still needed a few bucks for the rent, the boatman, and all that *barter* shit ... and, like, to go back would be a total, mind-blowing downer ... the *clinics*, and the *pollution* ... the *hostility* of the pigs and the landlords and the freaks and the uptight straight world. And wow, to have to wait an *hour* on a cold *night* for a bus, and make *three* transfers, to get somewhere that would take ten minutes by car ... and to have Moonbeam getting her head fucked with the Pledge of Allegiance, and marching to recess in lines, and having to raise her hand if she wanted to talk, or pee ... wow, we couldn't go back to all that 'urban-poor' crap, we just *couldn't!*

We went down into a really deep bummer that lasted all

the rest of that day and night. Our auras were really dimmed-out, and our minds were low, man, really low.

The next morning we decided that the best thing to do would be to get super-stoned, and maybe that would put our heads in a better place, so we could figure out what to do. We decided to make it into the bush and score some more of those 'poison' mushrooms that Brother Jo had turned us onto.

We told everyone we felt like a little stroll. 'Mind de sun,' warned Miz Rose, when we laid Moonbeam on her. We got into the bush and did a little search trip, and found a little patch of the mushrooms under a huge, flowering bush.

'Like we want to get really *loaded*, this time, right?' asked my old man, and he reached down and grabbed a couple of great big mushrooms and popped them into his mouth. I did the same, and we crawled under the bush, digging the sticky heat and the jungly noises and smells. We had that waiting feeling, like before something starts to work, but like, there's no doubt when this stuff hits you ... *phew*....

And like there we were, again in the magic land of green, with all those funny little comic-strip characters balling and doing their things ... but this time we didn't just stay there....

This time our heads got into a new place ... a very clear place ... the greens were still there, but like we could *see* all the jungle sights and *smell* all the jungle smells and *hear* all noises, like we were some kind of animal or something. And I looked at my old man and, well shit, you really get some *weird* hallucinations on this stuff, because he looked all furry, like, and his hands and feet looked kind of like a duck's! I told him that, and he opened his eyes ... they looked enormous and green, like pearly jade ... and he giggled and said, 'Wow, you look like that, too. Metamorphosis....' But I wasn't too sure it was funny, cause usually you can *tell* what's a hallucination and what isn't, but this time I *couldn't*. It kind of freaked me, but I didn't want to say anything that might put him on a bummer.

After a few hours, we got up and walked around. The air felt surprisingly nice and cool, and we were really tripping out on all the sounds and sights and smells which we never imagined *existed* before.

We ate some fruit, but mostly we felt really hungry for some more of those mushrooms, so we ate some, but they didn't get us any higher, just kept us in the same place ... well into the night, when we found that we were really into seeing in the dark.

Animals and snakes came near us and didn't seem to be on any hostility or fear trips. We petted them and fed them some fruit and really grooved with their vibes. Finally we curled up under a bush and went to sleep, figuring we'd surely be down by tomorrow, and looking our usual selves.

But the next morning we were as high as ever and I was getting kind of scared ... like how were we going to *stay* this way? With everything so high and clear and hallucinating that we were one of Brother Jo's fairy tales?

We figured that we'd better fall by his hut so he could give us something to make us come down, so we found our way to the edge of the village and tiptoed quietly inside. Some of Miz Rose's daughters were there, getting ointment rubbed on their backs, but when they saw us in the doorway they started to *jabber* and *bellow* and *throw* things at us like we were King Kong or something!

'*De do-do-mon!* Brother Jo, de do-do-mon come here! Hurry now, give us something for de do-do-mon!' Brother Jo didn't understand them at first, but finally he did, and got just as freaked out and started fumbling for some of that bark he gave everyone before the crab hunt. When they swallowed it, we began to smell the most horribly nauseating, corpse-sweet smell, that made us retch and feel dizzy and sick as all hell. We ran out of there, and they ran after us, throwing anything they could get their hands on ... and their aim was too fucking good!

We ran back into the cool and friendly bush and crawled under some high grasses to vomit and rub our bruises, until we felt more or less okay again, though kind of shaken up.

And like we still didn't come down. We figured we'd better

quit eating the mushrooms, even though we were craving them ... and we waited a while but ... we still looked the same.

We still didn't come down.

Well, shit, our heads have gone through a lot of changes about it since then. It's been over a month now, and for a while we were really bum-tripped about the whole thing ... especially my old man.

'You can't be a revolutionary when you're looking like a goddamn platypus,' he kept saying. But after a while he stopped worrying too much about the revolution ... like it really isn't important out here in the bush.

Then we started thinking how it would be kind of funny if we tried to go back to San Francisco and collect our welfare checks. That would really blow their minds ... they could use us as 'perfect examples of drug abuse' ... but we don't much need our welfare checks here. We've got the mushrooms and fruit, bushes to sleep and ball under ... and we can spend our time watching all the green ... the endless shades of green....

Anyway, we couldn't have stayed in the village with no bread for rent or chocolate bars 'n' shit ... and it would've really killed us to go back to the dead-end, head-fucking scene in the States. And, ya know, after we'd been out here a while, we started to lose a lot of that artificial brain-trip stuff that had been programmed into us since we were kids. Reading, writing ... like, when you don't use it, it just goes away. Like we're so much into the here and now that we don't much miss it. We're getting into a heavy telepathy trip with the animals, insects, even the plants ... this furry stuff keeps us nice and cool, and the webbed feet makes swimming kind of a gas. I don't much care about all that 'abstract,' human shit anymore ... like I really wasn't making it too well in *their* world.

The one problem is that we're kind of lonely here, just me and my old man. There are others out here like us, but they're pretty hard to rap with ... they just sit and stare and eat the mushrooms ... really spaced out.

My old man says, 'If we could remember how to write, we could write to our social worker, Phil, to come and join us ... if there was any paper out here ... or stamps ... or mailboxes.'

We've tried to go back to the village a few times and rap with the brothers and sisters there ... let them know there's nothing to be afraid of ... but, wow, they won't even *listen!* They just freak out, eat that goddamn, awful smelling bark and chase after us with machetes ... and how much can we take of those bad vibes?

There is one thing that'll make me feel better, and I intend to do something about it real soon. The next time there's a dark night with no moon, I'm going to sneak into the village and get little Moonbeam. I'm sure Miz Rose has been treating her real fine, but I want her out here with *me* ... her funny, giggling ways would make such fine company. I can feed her some of the mushrooms. (What was it Brother Jo said? The do-do-mon takes children who have lost their parents ... and if they eat what the do-do-mon gives them, then he keeps them, but if they won't eat it, then the do-do-mon has to let them go ... right on, Brother Jo.) But I know I can get Moonbeam to eat some of the mushrooms ... she's such a trusting little chickie. Then she could groove right along with us. She'd really dig it ... really trip out on all the green ... all the endless prisms of green....

Sky

R. A. LAFFERTY

THE SKY-SELLER was Mr. Furtive himself, fox-muzzled, ferret-eyed, slithering along like a snake, and living under the Rocks. The Rocks had not been a grand place for a long time. It had been built in the grand style on a mephitic plot of earth (to transform it), but the mephitic earth had won out. The apartments of the Rocks had lost their sparkle as they had been divided again and again, and now they were shoddy. The Rocks had weathered. Its once pastel hues were now dull grays and browns.

The five underground levels had been parking places for motor vehicles when those were still common, but now these depths were turned into warrens and hovels. The Sky-Seller lurked and lived in the lowest and smallest and meanest of them all.

He came out only at night. Daylight would have killed him: he knew that. He sold out of the darkest shadows of the night. He had only a few (though oddly select) clients, and nobody knew who his supplier was. He said that he had no supplier, that he gathered and made the stuff himself.

Welkin Alauda, a full-bodied but light-moving girl (it was said her bones were hollow and filled with air), came to the Sky-Seller just before first light, just when he had become highly nervous but had not yet bolted to his underground.

'A sack of Sky from the nervous mouse. Jump, or the sun will gobble your house!' Welkin sang-song, and she was already higher than most skies.

'Hurry, hurry!' the Sky-Seller begged, thrusting the sack to

her while his black eyes trembled and glittered (if real light should ever reflect into them he'd go blind).

Welkin took the sack of Sky, and scrambled money notes into his hands which had furred palms. (Really? Yes, really.)

'World be flat and the Air be round, wherever the Sky grows underground,' Welkin intoned, taking the sack of Sky and soaring along with a light scamper of feet (she hadn't much weight, her bones were hollow). And the Sky-Seller darted head-first down a black well-shaft thing to his depths.

Four of them went Sky-Diving that morning, Welkin herself, Karl Vlieger, Icarus Riley, Joseph Alzarsi; and the pilot was – (no, not who you think, he had already threatened to turn them all in; they'd use that pilot no more) – the pilot was Ronald Kolibri in his little crop-dusting plane.

But a crop-duster will not go up to the frosty heights they liked to take off from. Yes it will – if everybody is on Sky. But it isn't pressurized, and it doesn't carry oxygen. That doesn't matter, not if everybody is on Sky, not if the plane is on Sky too.

Welkin took Sky with Mountain Whizz, a carbonated drink. Karl stuffed it into his lip like snuff. Icarus Riley rolled it and smoked it. Joseph Alzarsi needled it, mixed with drinking alcohol, into his main vein. The pilot Ronny tongued and chewed it like sugar dust. The plane named Shrike took it through the manifold.

Fifty thousand feet— You can't go that high in a crop-duster. Thirty below zero— Ah, that isn't cold! Air too thin to breathe at all – with Sky, who needs such included things as air?

Welkin stepped out, and went up, not down. It was a trick she often pulled. She hadn't much weight; she could always get higher than the rest of them. She went up and up until she disappeared. Then she drifted down again, completely enclosed in a sphere of ice crystal, sparkling inside it and making monkey-faces at them.

The wind yelled and barked, and the divers took off. They all went down, soaring and gliding and tumbling; standing still sometimes, it seemed; even rising again a little. They went down to clouds and spread out on them: black-white clouds with the sun inside them and suffusing them both from above and below. They cracked Welkin's ice-crystal sphere and she stepped out of it. They ate the thin pieces of it, very cold and brittle and with a tang of ozone. Alzarsi took off his shirt and sunned himself on a cloud.

'You will burn,' Welkin told him. 'Nobody burns so as when sunning himself on a cloud.' That was true.

They sank through the black-whiteness of these clouds and came into the limitless blue concourse with clouds above and below them. It was in this same concourse that Hippodameia used to race her horses, there not being room for such coursers to run on earth. The clouds below folded up and the clouds above folded down, forming a discrete space.

'We have our own rotundity and sphere here,' said Icarus Riley (these are their Sky-Diver names, not their legal names), 'and it is apart from all worlds and bodies. The worlds and the bodies do not exist for as long a time as we say that they do not exist. The axis of our present space is its own concord. Therefore, it being in perfect concord, Time stops.'

All their watches had stopped, at least.

'But there *is* a world below,' said Karl. 'It is an abject world, and we can keep it abject forever if we wish. But it has at least a shadowy existence, and later we will let it fill out again in our compassion for lowly things. It is flat, though, and we must insist that it remain flat.'

'This is important,' Joseph said with the deep importance of one on Sky. 'So long as our own space is bowed and globed, the world must remain flat or depressed. But the world must not be allowed to bow its back again. We are in danger if it ever does. So long as it is truly flat and abject it cannot crash ourselves to it.'

'How long could we fall,' Welkin asked, 'if we had not stopped time, if we let it flow at its own pace, or at ours? How long could we fall?'

'Hephaestus once tumbled through space all day long,' Icarus Riley said, 'and the days were longer then.'

Karl Vlieger had gone wall-eyed from an interior-turned sexual passion that he often experienced in diving. Icarus Riley seemed to be on laughing gas suddenly; this is a sign that Sky is not having perfect effect. Joseph Alzarsi felt a cold wind down his spine and a series of jerky little premonitions.

'We are not perfect,' Joseph said. 'Tomorrow or the next day we may be, for we *do* approach perfection. We win a round. And we win another. Let us not throw away our victory today through carelessness. The earth has bowed his old back a little bit, and we make ready for him! Now, guys, now!'

Four of them (or maybe only three of them) pulled the rings. The chutes unpeeled, flowered, and jerked. They had been together like a sheaf in close conversation. But suddenly, on coming to earth, they were spread out over five hundred yards.

They assembled. They packed their chutes. That would be all the diving for that day.

'Welkin, how did you pack your chute so quickly?' Icarus asked her suspiciously.

'I don't know.'

'You are always the slowest one of us, and the sloppiest. Someone always has to re-roll your chute for you before it is used again. And you were the last one to land just now. How were you the first one to be packed? How did you roll it so well? It has the earmarks of my own rolling, just as I rolled it for you before we took off this morning.'

'I don't know, Icarus. Oh, I think I'll go up again, straight up.'

'No, you've sailed and dived enough for one morning. Welkin, did you even open your chute?'

'I don't know.'

High on Sky, they went up again the next morning. The little plane named Shrike flew up as no plane had ever flown before, up through Storm. The storm-shrouded earth shrank to the size of a pea-doogie.

'We will play a trick on it,' said Welkin. 'When you're on Sky you can play a trick on anything and make it abide by it. I will say that the pea-doogie that was the world is nothing. See, it is gone. Then I will select another pea-doogie, that one there, and I will call it the world. And that *is* the world that we will come down to in a little while. I've switched worlds on the world, and it doesn't know what happened to it.'

'It's uneasy, though.' Joseph Alzarsi spoke through flared nostrils. 'You shook it. No wonder the world has its moments of self-doubt.'

They were one million feet high. The altimeter didn't go that high, but Ronald Kolibri the pilot wrote out the extended figure in chalk to make it correct. Welkin stepped out. Karl and Icarus and Joseph stepped out. Ronald Kolibri stepped out, but only for a while. Then he remembered that he was the pilot and got back in the plane. They were so high that the air was black and star-filled instead of blue. It was so cold that the empty space was full of cracks and potholes. They dived half a million feet in no time at all. They pulled up laughing.

It was invigorating, it was vivifying. They stamped on the clouds, and the clouds rang like frosty ground. This was the ancestral country of all hoarfrost, of all grained-snow and glare-ice. Here was weather-maker, here was wind-son. They came into caves of ice mixed with moraine; they found antler hatchets and Hemicyon bones; they found coals still glowing. The winds bayed and hunted in packs through the chasms. These were the cold Fortean clouds, and their location is commonly quite high.

They came down below Storm, finding new sun and new air. It was pumpkin-summer, it was deep autumn in the sky.

They dropped again, miles and millennia, to full Sky-summer: the air so blue that it grew a violet patina on it to save the surface. Their own space formed about them again, as it did every day, and time stopped.

But not motion! Motion never stopped with them. Do you not realize that nothingness in a void can still be in motion? And how much more they of the great centrality! There was Dynamic; there was sustaining vortex; there was the high serenity of fevered motion.

But is not motion merely a relationship of space to time? No. That is an idea that is common to people who live on worlds, but it is a subjective idea. Here, beyond the possible influence of any worlds, there was living motion without reference.

'Welkin, you look quite different today,' Joseph Alzarsi spoke in wonder. 'What is it?'

'I don't know. It's wonderful to be different and I'm wonderful.'

'It is something missing from you,' said Icarus. 'I believe it is a defect missing.'

'But I hadn't any, Icarus.'

They were in central and eternal moment, and it did not end, it could not end, it goes on yet. Whatever else seems to happen, it is merely in parentheses to that moment.

'It is time to consider again,' Icarus mused after a while. There is no time or while in the Moment, but there is in the parentheses. 'I hope it is the last time we will ever have to consider. We, of course, are in our own space and beyond time or tangent. But the earth, such as it is, is approaching with great presumption and speed.'

'But it's *nothing* to us!' Karl Vlieger suddenly raged out in a chthonic and phallic passion. 'We can shatter it! We can shoot it to pieces like a clay pigeon! It cannot rush onto us like a slashing dog. Get down, world! Heel, you cur! Heel, I say!'

'We say to one world "rise" and it rises, and to another one "heel" and it heels,' Icarus sky-spoke in his dynamic serenity.

'Not yet,' Joseph Alzarsi warned. 'Tomorrow we will be total. Today we are not yet. Possibly we *could* shatter the world like a clay pigeon if we wished, but we would not be lords of it if we had to shatter it.'

'We could always make another world,' said Welkin reasonably.

'Certainly, but this one is our testing. We will go to it when it is crouched down. We cannot allow it to come ravening to us. Hold! Hold there, we order you!'

And the uprushing world halted, cowed.

'We go down,' said Joseph. 'We will let it come up only when it is properly broken.'

('And they inclined the heavens and came down.')

Once more, three of them pulled the rings. And the chutes unpeeled, flowered, and jerked. They had been like a sheaf together in their moment; but now, coming to earth, they were suddenly scattered out over five hundred yards.

'Welkin, you didn't have your chute at all today!' Icarus gaped with some awe when they had assembled again. 'That is what was different about you.'

'No, I guess I didn't have it. There was no reason to have it if I didn't need it. Really, there was never any reason for me to have used one at all ever.'

'Ah, we *were* total today and didn't know it,' Joseph ventured. 'Tomorrow none of us will wear chutes. This is easier than I had believed.'

Welkin went to the Sky-Seller to buy new Sky that night. Not finding him in the nearer shadows of the Rocks, she went down and down, drawn by the fungoid odor and the echoing dampness of the underground. She went through passages that were man-made, through passages that were natural, through passages that were unnatural. Some of these corridors, it is true, had once been built by men, but now they had reverted and become most unnatural deep-earth caverns. Welkin went down into the total blackness where there were certain small things that still mumbled out a faint white color; but it was the wrong color white, and the things were all of a wrong shape.

There was the dead white shape of Mycelium masses, the grotesqueness of Agaricus, the deformity of Deadly Amanita and of Morel. The gray-milky Lactarius glowed like lightless lanterns in the dark; there was the blue-white of the Deceiving Clitocybe and the yellow-white of the Caesar Agaric. There was the insane ghost-white of the deadliest and queerest of them all, the Fly Amanita, and a mole was gathering this.

'Mole, bring Sky for the Thing Serene, for the Minions tall and the Airy Queen,' Welkin jangled. She was still high on Sky, but it had begun to leave her a little and she had the veriest touch of the desolate sickness.

'Sky for the Queen of the buzzing drones, with her hollow heart and her hollow bones,' the Sky-Seller intoned hollowly.

'And fresh, Oh I want it fresh, fresh Sky!' Welkin cried.

'With these creatures there is no such thing as fresh,' the Sky-Seller told her. 'You want it stale, Oh so stale! Ingrown and aged and with its own mold grown moldy.'

'Which is it?' Welkin demanded. 'What is the name of the one you gather it from?'

'The Fly Amanita.'

'But isn't that simply a poisonous mushroom?'

'It has passed beyond that. It has sublimated. Its simple poison has had its second fermenting into narcotic.'

'But it sounds so cheap that it be merely narcotic.'

'Not merely narcotic. It is something very special in narcotic.'

'No, no, not narcotic at all!' Welkin protested. 'It is liberating, it is world-shattering. It is Height Absolute. It is motion and detachment itself. It is the ultimate. It is mastery.'

'Why, then it is mastery, lady. It is the highest and lowest of all created things.'

'No, no,' Welkin protested again, 'not created. It is not born, it is not made. I couldn't stand that. It is the highest of all uncreated things.'

'Take it, take it,' the Sky-Seller growled, 'and be gone. Something begins to curl up inside me.'

'I go!' Welkin said, 'and I will be back many times for more.'

'No, you will not be. Nobody ever comes back many times for Sky. You will be back never. Or one time. I think that you will be back one time.'

They went up again the next morning, the last morning. But why should we say that it was the last morning? Because there would no longer be divisions or days for them. It would be one last eternal day for them now, and nothing could break it.

They went up in the plane that had once been named Shrike and was now named Eternal Eagle. The plane had repainted itself during the night with new name and new symbols, some of them not immediately understandable. The plane snuffled Sky into its manifolds, and grinned and roared. And the plane went up.

Oh! Jerusalem in the Sky! How it went up!

They were all certainly perfect now and would never need Sky again. *They were Sky.*

'How little the world is!' Welkin rang out. 'The towns are like fly-specks and the cities are like flies.'

'It is wrong that so ignoble a creature as the Fly should have the exalted name,' Icarus complained.

'I'll fix that,' Welkin sang. 'I give edict: That all the flies on earth be dead!' And all the flies on earth died in that instant.

'I wasn't sure you could do that,' said Joseph Alzarsi. 'The wrong is righted. Now we ourselves assume the noble name of Flies. There are no Flies but us!'

The five of them, including the pilot Ronald Kolibri, stepped chuteless out of the Eternal Eagle.

'Will you be all right?' Ronald asked the rollicking plane.

'Certainly,' the plane said. 'I believe I know where there are other Eternal Eagles. I will mate.'

It was cloudless, or else they had developed the facility of seeing through clouds. Or perhaps it was that, the earth having become as small as a marble, the clouds around it were insignificant.

Pure light that had an everywhere source! (The sun also had become insignificant and didn't contribute much to the light.) Pure and intense motion that had no location reference. They weren't going anywhere with their intense motion (they already *were* everywhere, or at the super-charged center of everything).

Pure cold fever. Pure serenity. Impure hyper-space passion of Karl Vlieger, and then of all of them; but it was purely rampant at least. Stunning beauty in all things along with a towering cragginess that was just ugly enough to create an ecstasy.

Welkin Alauda was mythic with nenuphars in her hair. And

it shall not be told what Joseph Alzarsi wore in his own hair. An always-instant, a million or a billion years!

Not monotony, no! Presentation! Living sets! Scenery! The scenes were formed for the splinter of a moment; or they were formed forever. Whole worlds formed in a pregnant void: not spherical worlds merely, but dodeka-spherical, and those much more intricate than that. Not merely seven colors to play with, but seven to the seventh and to the seventh again.

Stars vivid in the bright light. You who have seen stars only in darkness be silent! Asteroids that they ate like peanuts, for now they were all metamorphic giants. Galaxies like herds of rampaging elephants. Bridges so long that both ends of them receded over the light-speed edges. Waterfalls, of a finer water, that bounced off galaxy clusters as if they were boulders.

Through a certain ineptitude of handling, Welkin extinguished the old sun with one such leaping torrent.

'It does not matter,' Icarus told her. 'Either a million or a billion years had passed according to the time-scale of the bodies, and surely the sun had already come onto dim days. You can always make other suns.'

Karl Vlieger was casting lightning bolts millions of parsecs long and making looping contact with clustered galaxies with them.

'Are you sure that we are not using up any time?' Welkin asked them with some apprehension.

'Oh, time still uses itself up, but we are safely out of the reach of it all,' Joseph explained. 'Time is only one very inefficient method of counting numbers. It is inefficient because it is limited in its numbers, and because the counter by such a system must die when he has come to the end of his series. That alone should weigh against it as a mathematical system; it really shouldn't be taught.'

'Then nothing can hurt us ever?' Welkin wanted to be reassured.

'No, nothing can come at us except inside time and we are outside it. Nothing can collide with us except in space and we disdain space. Stop it, Karl! As you do it that's buggery.'

'I have a worm in my own tract and it gnaws at me a little,' the pilot Ronald Kolibri said. 'It's in my internal space and it's crunching along at a pretty good rate.'

'No, no, that's impossible. Nothing can reach or hurt us,' Joseph insisted.

'I have a worm of my own in a still more interior tract,' said Icarus, 'the tract that they never quite located in the head or the heart or the bowels. Maybe this tract always was outside space. Oh, my worm doesn't gnaw, but it stirs. Maybe I'm tired of being out of reach of everything.'

'Where do these doubts rise from?' Joseph sounded querulous. 'You hadn't them an instant ago, you hadn't them as recently as ten million years ago. How can you have them now when there isn't any now?'

'Well, as to that –' Icarus began – (and a million years went by) – 'as to that I have a sort of cosmic curiosity about an object in my own past' – (another million years went by) – 'an object called world.'

'Well, satisfy your curiosity then,' Karl Vlieger snapped. 'Don't you even know how to make a world?'

'Certainly I know how, but will it be the same?'

'Yes, if you're good enough. It will be the same if you make it the same.'

Icarus Riley made a world. He wasn't very good at it and it wasn't quite the same, but it did resemble the old world a little.

'I want to see if some things are still there,' Welkin clamored. 'Bring it closer.'

'It's unlikely your things are still there,' Joseph said. 'Remember that billions of years may have passed.'

'The things will be there if I put them there,' Icarus insisted.

'And you cannot bring it closer since all distance is now infinite,' Karl maintained.

'At least I can focus it better.' Icarus insisted, and he did. The world appeared quite near.

'It remembers us like a puppy would,' Welkin said. 'See, it jumps up at us.'

'It's more like a lion leaping for a treed hunter just out of reach,' Icarus grudged. 'But we are *not* treed.'

'It can't ever reach us, and it wants to,' Welkin piqued. 'Let's reach down to it.'

('And they inclined the heavens and went down.')

A most peculiar thing happened to Ronald Kolibri as he touched earth. He seemed to have a seizure. He went slack-faced, almost horror-faced, and he would not answer the others.

'What is it, Ronald?' Welkin begged in kindred anguish. 'Oh, what is it? Somebody help him!'

Then Ronald Kolibri did an even more peculiar thing. He began to fold up and break up from the bottom. Bones slowly splintered and pierced out of him and his entrails gushed out. He compressed. He shattered. He splashed. Can a man splash?

The same sort of seizure overtook Karl Vlieger: the identical slack-face horror-face, the same folding up and breaking up from the bottom, the same hideous sequence.

And Joseph Alzarsi went into the same sundering state, baffled and breaking up.

'Icarus, what's happened to them?' Welkin screamed. 'What is the slow loud booming?'

'They're dead. How could that be?' Icarus puzzled trembling. 'Death is in time, and we are not.'

Icarus himself passed through time as he crashed earth, breaking up, spilling out more odiously than any of them.

And Welkin touched earth, crashed, then what? She heard her own slow loud booming as she hit.

(Another million years went by, or some weeks.)

A shaky old woman on crutches was going down the middle-of-the-night passages that are under the Rocks. She was too old a woman to be Welkin Alauda, but not too old for a Welkin who had lived millions of years outside of time.

She had not died. She was lighter than the others, and besides she had done it twice before unscathed. But that was before she had known fear.

Naturally they had told her that she would never walk again; and now most unnaturally she was walking with crutches. Drawn by the fungoid odor and the echoing dampness she went down in the total dark to where small things were growing with the wrong color white and were all of the wrong shape. She wanted one thing only, and she would die without it.

'Sky for salving the broken Crone! Sky for the weal of my hollow bone!' she crackled in an old-woman voice. But it was only her own voice that echoed back to her.

Should a Sky-Seller live forever?

All of Them Were Empty –

DAVID GERROLD

IN A city of night and neon. She had puppy-soft eyes and an old army coat. I had a sweatshirt and levis and an acid-laced joint. We watched the colors smear.

We sheared our eyes on the slashing lights and let them bleed into the streets. The lights. Glowworm letters and gray crumbling walls.

My blood was copper, hers was gold; I was strong and red, she was soft and malleable.

She had sucking eyes. They could eat you up, or they could tease. Black whirlpool pupils, large and moist.

I moved like stone down the hollow deathwalk, the tall night above, the close city around. The unreal-colored neon flashed us messages of EAT, DRINK and JESUS SAVES. She moved with me like a wraith, a shadow of a girl suspended in air, attached to my jacket, following ghostlike and effortless. 'Deet?' she said, and her voice was like that first big hit – painful, elusive and narcotic.

'Deet?' she asked again. 'Let's go home, huh?'

A shake of my head. 'Not yet, Wooze; not yet.' Wooze, short for Woozle.

'But I'm tired, Deet. It's my period and I don't feel good.'

'Then go.'

'I don't want to go alone.'

'Then don't go.'

'Deet . . .' she said plaintively. I looked at her; she was using *that* tone of voice again. She shut.

'Nobody asked you to come,' I said.

'I don't like to be by myself. I want to stay with you.'

'Okay, then stay. But if you're going to talk about going home, I'm gonna ditch you.'

'You wouldn't.'

'Want to find out?'

She didn't answer, instead pulled her coat tighter about her, shoved skinny hands into skinny pockets and cringed against the city. Cars like giant panthers prowled the night streets, rolling silent-rumbly through dark-lit intersections and wet gutter bottoms. Eyes glowing, they spotlit their prey in white-lined cross-walks and rushed eagerly toward them, only to be cheated when the lone figures vanished into the safety of the soft black buildings.

Doors like hungry mouths pulled at us. She half-ran, half-walked to keep up with me. 'Deet? Where we going anyway?'

'To a place.'

'You said that before, Deet. Which place? We going to Cannie's?'

I shook my head. 'Not Cannie's. I don't like his stuff.'

'You used to.'

'Not any more. Got something new.'

'A new place?'

'A new place, yeah.' Hands in my pockets, tight-wrapped around a narrow roll of bills. Yeah, a new place. And new stuff.

Got to get away from the old stuff. Clot your mind. Too many pills, your eyes turn to glass, shatter with the morning. Your stomach turns to liquid, bleeds away in the night.

Two ways to go. Up or down. Down, back into the brightlit land of the straights – or up, into the pastel razorblade world of H. H for heavy stuff, for hard stuff.

Uh uh, not me. Not H. H is for hooked. Seen the cold turkey once too often. Not H.

But still, two ways to go. Up or down.

Tried them all, speed, mesc, acid. Acid's okay and mesc is a people trip. But speed is the deathman. Speed kills, comes after you with the crystal knife shining.

Still, you got to make the choice, Deet; can't stand still – up or down?

– or why not *out*?

Why not a whole new direction? Hang a sudden left and leave them all. A whole new kick. Who said it had to be *this* or *that*? Why does it have to be either? Yeah, I had it. I had it now. I knew the way.

To hell with up or down. What's wrong with right and left and north and east and yesterday and Tuesday and Charlie and purple and?

I knew the way. All I had to do was find it. I didn't have the address though. All I had was a description of where it was, and I still had to go looking for it.

Woozle was woozy. She kept wiping her nose on her sleeve. It was red; so were her eyes. 'You crying again?'

'Uh uh, Deet. I wouldn't do that. Uh uh. I got a cold, that's all. I told you, it's my period.'

'That gives you a cold?'

'Yes. No. I don't know.' She shrugged her baggy-green coat around her shouders. 'Deet, I'm awfully tired. Could we sit down a minute?'

'We're almost there.'

'Where? We aren't anywhere. . . .'

'We're almost there. Don't worry about it.'

She sat down anyway. All right; I stopped and waited. The streets shone in the dark. Like water. Dark puddles from the rain lapped at the curbs. I lit the last joint, inhaled deep, deep, deep, sharp pain, and deeper, deep hit. Acid-laced hit. Yeah.

I wanted to hallucinate. Another hit. I could feel it coming.

I offered Woozle the joint. She shook her head. 'Uh uh. Not any more, Deet. I'm afraid I'll go on a bad trip.'

I already was. I took another. Yeah, that was it.

A car came floating down the street, cleaving water to either side of its bow, cleaving an inky wake. I was glad we were on this side of the street. I didn't want to swim the canal tonight. I wondered where the horses were.

Did they still put running lights on them? I wondered. On

what, I asked, but I couldn't remember.

The joint disappeared back into a baggie, flame pinched out first, then into the underwear. Nestled tight, a nice place to keep things.

The door was where I had left it. Knocked.

No answer. Knocked it again.

An eye, red like the cherry on a copcar, peered out. 'Yeah?'

'Deet. My name's Deet.'

'Yeah? So what?'

'Told to come by.'

'By who?' the eye demanded, floating behind a black wall.

'You did. Somebody did. Said something about a new kick or something.'

'What'd you say your name was?'

'Deet.'

The eye swiveled around to look at the Woozle. 'What's that?'

'She's with me.'

'She okay?'

'I said, she's with me.'

'Who sent you?'

'I don't know his name. Their names.'

'Who's they?'

'A guy – no, two guys. And a girl. Strange girl. Pale eyes.'

'Tamra?'

'That could be it. Yeah, that's it. That's who it was. Tamra.'

'Uh uh – no Tamra. We got no Tamra.' The eye started to close.

'Hey!'

It opened again.

'Hey, man – what is this? You guys told me to come by here—'

'Where'd we tell you?'

'Here!'

'No, where were we when we told you?'

'Cannie's.'

'Where's that?'

I told him.

'Wait.' The eye closed.

We waited.

Night waited. The street lights seeped and sucked at the dark. It sucked back. Somewhere a thing splashed through the waves.

The eye opened. 'All right.'

We went in. It was redlit, like the churchman's Hell. A naked red bulb sat on top of the room, not bright enough to light, dim enough to be painful. Everything was a red blur.

Woozle took one look and groaned. She covered her eyes and grabbed at my jacket with an unsteady hand. She hung onto me all the while, following with one hand over her eyes. Well, she'd asked to come; it wasn't my fault.

The guy – yeah, it was a guy – had hair of barbed wire brillo, a dark scraggly bush. Eyes like a prowl car. Heavy. He was wearing only shapeless underwear and a paint-stained blanket-poncho. It didn't cover much.

'This way,' he said.

We pad-padded down a long corridor. The place was one of those narrow apartments that shows only a door to the street and stretches forever inland. Narrow rooms, narrow rooms, one after the other, open and empty. Some mattresses, an old box, a blanket, the remains of a shirt, scraps of paper, floors and walls. Nothing more. And everything redlit.

We went all the way to the back. One or two of the doors were closed, with sounds seeping out around the edges – once the sound of surf. But the ones I could see into were empty. Somewhere a record player tinkered with sounds and darkness.

The last room was like all the rest. Except something smelled funny. Like dusty orange. Two or three mattresses lay dirty on the floor. Four people in the room: two guys, two girls. They all had tombstone eyes. I didn't like the looks, but I'd heard about the new kick and I wanted to try it.

'This's Deet,' grunted the brillohead.

Casual glances, nothing more.

'That's Woozle,' I said, nodding at the Wooze. She was still covering her eyes.

'Sit,' shrugged one of the girls. I sat. Woozle, putting one hand behind her, lowered herself. The mattresses had no soft; they were flat and dusty-slimy.

The two guys were off to one side, sitting-leaning up against the wall and looking at each other. Okay, none of my business. It was the girls who held my attention. They had pale eyes, pink in the redlit room.

'Who are you?' one asked.

'Deet. I'm Deet. He just told you —' I pointed at brillohair, but he wasn't there anymore.

'Uh uh,' she shook her head. '*Who* are you?'

Shrug. 'I'm me. That's all.'

'Okay. Who's she?'

'She's Woozle. She goes where I go.'

'Everywhere?'

'Just about.'

'You like that?' Her voice was like an empty room. It echoed.

'Yeah, it's okay, I guess.'

'You don't like it?'

'I don't know,' I shrugged again. 'I'm used to it.'

'You want to change it?'

'Why should I?'

'Yes. Why *should* you?'

I wasn't sure what she was talking about any more. I shrugged. 'Why do you want to know?'

This time, she shrugged. 'Need to know. That's all.'

Woozle tugged at my arm then. I ignored it.

The other girl now, 'Where're you headed?'

'Nowhere now. We're here.'

'This is where you want to be?'

Another tug at the arm. I shook it off and answered the pale-eyed question, 'It's as good a place as any.'

'Deet . . .' said Woozle, and she had that tone again. Plaintive. '*Deet . . .!*'

'Christ, you're a nuisance, Woozle, you know that? What do you want?'

She pushed hair back out of her eyes, looked at me, wetly. 'Deet, I want to go home.'

'Then go, dammit!'

'Uh uh, Deet. Not without you. Deet, I'm scared.' She lowered her voice to a point where she was almost mouthing the words. 'Deet, these people scare me.'

'It's all right, Wooze. I'm here.'

'That's what I'm scared about. You're *here*. I don't think you should be.'

'You starting that again?'

She lowered her eyes. 'No. I'm sorry. It's just that—'

'Aw, look—' I knew she wanted me to touch her then, but I didn't. 'Look, this'll only take a minute. Promise. Then we'll go. Okay?'

She looked up with tear streaks. 'Promise?'

'Promise,' I said, and touched her chin. 'Just don't nag me, okay?'

'Okay, Deet. I'm sorry.' She sniffed at her sleeve.

I looked back at the girls. They had long stringy hair; like they were hiding behind it. There was something funny about the shapes of their mouths too. I smiled, sort of, as if to excuse the Woozle.

They didn't smile back. Okay, I didn't care. They took up their questioning where they left off. Questioning? What was this anyway – a test? Why did I have to pass a test?

'Hey,' I interrupted. 'I didn't come to talk. I came for the kick.'

'We know. You'll get it. But it's . . . uncool to just kick and run. You've got to talk to us first. We like to talk.'

'I don't.' I looked at their eyes.

'But we do,' they answered patiently.

'Look, I got the cash for it – just give it to me and we'll go.'

'Don't want cash,' said one.

'Want you,' said the other.

'Huh?' I said.

And, 'Deet!' said Woozle. 'Let's get out of here.'

I ignored the voice at my sleeve. 'What're you talking about?'

'We want you. To talk to. That's our price.'

'Oh. I thought you meant something else.'

'Uh uh,' she said.

'Good. That's not my bag.'

'Not ours either.' She rearranged herself on the mattress. They looked at me again. Hungry. Patient bitches, weren't they?

'What is your thing?' they asked.

'I don't know. Just being me, I guess.'

'But who are you? Do you know?'

I shook my head. To clear it. It wasn't making sense any more. If it ever did. 'Hey, enough of this already. Where's the hit I came for?'

'We're giving it to you,' said one.

'We're trying to give it to you,' said the other.

'Right now,' added the first.

'Uh uh,' I shook my head. 'Uh uh, I'm not buying a shuck. I haven't smoked anything. I haven't dropped anything. So far, all we've done is talk —'

'Yes, yes,' she had a voice like a movie geisha, all treble and no bass. 'That's it. A *communicating* . . . thing.'

'Huh? I don't —' I mean, it doesn't.

She cocked her head, 'It is essential that —'

Something was wrong, the whole thing was all tilty-slidy and kept creeping off at the edges. I tried to yank it back, but it wouldn't. Somehow I kept missing the undertones.

They were ignoring me. They were looking at each other and talking softly, words like, '. . . doesn't want . . . needs a tangible . . .'

The first one shook her head, as if in disagreement, '. . . *does* want . . .'

'. . . doesn't . . .'

'. . . *does* . . . just doesn't know that he . . .'

The second one shook her head now, 'No ... needs a tan gibble ... trib won't work unless ... must believes ...'

The first one nodded at that, 'Yes ... is necessary ... give something ...'

The second one made a suggestion.

The first one glanced up sharply. '... not ...'

The second one: '... what else ... trib is trib ... he wants ... we give ...'

'Trib is not trib ... this bite is ...'

'Bite is bite is bite ...' snapped the second. 'Want not hear about it ...'

'Possibility for ickle-ickle-ickle ...'

'Am aware ... am aware ... am aware ...'

'Rather try communicor again ...' insisted the first.

'Won't work ... won't work ... doesn't want ... doesn't want ...' The second one seemed to have the upper hand in whatever it was. At last, the first one gave in and they looked at me, 'Okay. We give.'

'Great. What do we do? Smoke it? Drink it? Eat it?'

'None of those,' they shook their heads.

'Then how—?'

'Rub it on,' said one. The other was burrowing around under the mattress. 'Take off your clothes,' she said.

'Huh?'

'Take off your clothes. That's what you have to do.'

'You're not putting me on?'

'You want the hit?'

'Are you going to take one too?'

They shook their heads. 'We're already on ours. We don't need yours.'

'Oh.' I still didn't move to drop my clothes.

They waited. 'Are you shy?'

'No. It's just that—'

'Would you like us to take off our clothes too?' one asked. The other didn't wait for me to answer, but dropped her robe (how come I hadn't noticed that before?) to the floor. She was as sexless as an eight-year-old boy. Flat chested. I stared, yeah. No curves, nothing. What a bringdown. A super-bummer. A beautiful face like that and no bod. No hair, no nothing. The other was just the same, she'd dropped her robe too, only she was wearing black briefs. She didn't move to drop them. It wasn't necessary. My curiosity was dead.

'Well?' she asked.

'All right.' I shrugged out of my shirt, started to fumble with my belt. 'Hey, Wooze?'

'Yeah?'

'You coming?'

'Huh?'

'Take off your clothes ...'

'Uh uh, Deet. I don't want any. Thanks.'

'Aw, come on. I don't want to go alone.'

'No, Deet. All I want to do is go home.'

'Don't be a drag, Woozle. Do it.'

'I don't want to.'

'But I want you to.'

'Deet, I'll go anywhere you go, Deet. I'll never leave you alone. But please, don't ask me to take any more stuff, Deet. I don't like it.'

'How do you know? You haven't tried it.' I pulled her to her feet, started pulling her clothes off. She tried to resist at first, then realized it was useless. The army coat, the baggy jeans, the T-shirt and soiled underwear fell to the floor. She stood there naked and wiped her nose on the back of her wrist. 'Sit,' I said. She sat.

I kicked off my shoes, then dropped my pants and underwear all in one motion. Sit, lift the legs and slide them off; one foot, then the other. The two of us sat naked on the mattress. Ready for action. Whatever the action was.

Woozle was clenched in on herself, arms folded across tight little breasts. I don't know why she was ashamed. She had more than these girls did. No matter, she kept her nose into her knee and sniffed, wiped it across her leg.

I turned to the chicks. (What happened to the two guys who were in the room? Where did they go?) 'Okay, we're ready.'

One of them stepped forward (there was that funny smell again) and held out a jar that looked like a cold cream thing. I didn't take it.

First, I asked, 'How much?'

'Enough,' she replied. 'Enough for two.'

'No. I mean, how much do I owe you?'

She cocked her head in puzzlement, 'Nothing.'

'Uh uh,' I started to pick up my pants. 'No free rides. Not for this head.'

They exchanged a confused glance, 'Why?'

'Anything free's got a hook in it. Like the first jolt of H – and that's not my bag. Don't plan on getting hooked on anything.'

They looked at each other again. 'Okay. Twenty dollars.'

'Twenty?'

'Two rides. One yours, one hers.'

'Yeah,' but I was still suspicious.

'You want it? Or not?'

I sniffed. That was the source of the funny odor, like old orange peels. So were the girls. 'What is it?'

She shrugged, 'No name. Just is.'

'And I just rub it on.'

She nodded. She held the jar in her two hands and waited.

'No hook in it?'

'If you don't want it, we don't put hook in. Okay?'

'Okay,' I said slowly. 'No hook.' I still didn't like it, but I wanted to try it. The smell was getting deep, deeper. I wanted to feel what was at the bottom.

The decision was made. I pulled the twenty out of my pocket, creased it between my fingers to straighten it, and tossed it over. The jar was heavy in my hands and it had a slippery feel.

Okay, we'd do the number. Just once. See what it was and that'd be it. Course, that's what I'd said about acid the first time too. The top unscrewed greasy, and suddenly the funny smell was *intense*. It was sort of like ozone and sort of like flowers.

The girls were sitting again, hardly even watching. As if they'd lost all interest after making the connection. I turned to Wooze and offered the jar to her. She didn't look up. She didn't stand up.

'Just rub it in?' I asked.

'Uh huh,' said one of the girls. I couldn't tell which, I wasn't looking at them. 'All over. Cover everything you want to take with you.'

'Except the soles of your feet,' put in the other. 'Unless you don't want to come back.' And with that, they both laughed. I didn't get the joke. Perhaps I would later. I took some of the goop in my hand and smeared it across Woozle's chest. I had to go down on one knee and push her arms aside to do it. She didn't resist.

After a bit, I made her stand up and I made sure that I'd rubbed her all over – except for the soles of her feet. 'What's it feel like, Wooze?'

'Nothing yet. Just slippery.'

'Well, maybe it takes a little time. You do me now.'

She did. Her hands were dull and lifeless and spread the goop with no more feeling than shovels. She did it mechanically and uncaring, but she was thorough. I helped her a little bit, but it wasn't necessary. She was like a machine, running sensors all up and down me as if to memorize my body for later.

Then I was covered with the goop all over and the smell of it was overpowering. 'Now what?' I looked at the girls, but they weren't there.

'Hold hands,' they replied. 'That is, if you want to go together.'

Yeah, that sounded right. This was the new kick. This was what I'd been promised in front of Cannie's – a trip you could share. No more one-man-alone numbers. I was tired of sitting around in a room watching everybody else going in a different direction. I wanted someone to share my direction. Yeah, I was ready for it. Now, you could go and take someone good along to share it with you – and you could share theirs. I reached out for Woozle's hand. It felt different somehow. Tinier. Yeah, if you were going to share it, you should at least be holding hands.

I could feel the stuff now. Or, that is, I couldn't feel it any more. I couldn't feel anything any more. I felt ... *disembodied(?)* ... no, that wasn't it either. Creeping cold warmth was seeping out around my edges, dilating into the not-quite.

My eyes, great multi-faceted things, grew till they spread around the top and sides of my head and I looked in all directions at once. Woozle's hand looked back at mine. We stood half an inch above the floor and listened to water burning our legs.

What it was, was this – I was a pillar of fire, taken fresh from the freezer, standing still in the lightless and examining things in the reflected glare of (myself) and all was timeless until the water drops spattered into steam upon the hot. That didn't make sense.

But who cared? I was tripping. And Woozle was too. She was with me. She always was. Oh, yeah. We were in a tiny red cubicle – red from the frozen flame? – just one cubicle out of millions of identical tiny red cubicles stacked one upon another, left and right and north and east and yesterday and Tuesday and purple and —

FLASH!

Woop? What was that? Now the top of the room hung below us. We looked down the long tube at ourselves still holding hands. The red light seeped and pulsed and permeated it all. We were above and looking down and sideways at the little honeycombed rednesses below. Little black insects scraped within.

The whole city of shining black was below us. We looked down at them from our hot two-hundredth-story window, noses pressed flat against the glass, trying to push through it so as to see our own selves from the outside. Cannie's was only ten floors below. We watched the black uniforms herding them out of the building and into the street where they shot them. What a joke. Why hadn't it been listed in TV Guide?

Ooh, that was almost a bummer. We hopped the up elevator at the top floor and kept going and —

FLASH!

-ed again. What *was* that? Wow – whatever it was, it was. A desert hung below us. Above us. 'Oh, Wooze, look at that!'

She looked, 'Yeah, Deet, I see it.' Luminous fly-specks danced and skittered along a net of silver threads, in and out, patterns of streaking steel. Beyond it, the greater dark.

Another —

FLASH!

– and this time we're out in nothingness, looking at the whole marble. Why isn't it bigger? I thought it was bigger than that, didn't you? 'Hey, Deet – I mean, Woozle, isn't that supposed to be bigger?'

'I don't know, Deet. I'm just following you. Wherever you want, Deet.'

'Hey, don't be a bummer – this is ... *something*.'

Blue and white streaks, flat mottled brown patches, familiar shapes, but white streaks kept them from being too familiar and —

FLASH!

Now! I was starting to see the inside of it. It was like a whiteness, but with crystal blues and spidery blacks and all kinds of coldnesses creeping out from inside. An expanding – and a shrinking too.

'Deet! Please, slow down a bit. You're going too fast for me.'

'No, I'm not. It's okay.'

A greater darkness beyond, everything was scattered and speckled tiny this side of it. I wanted to expand to fill it. A glaring whiteness off to one side shouldn't have been that big. After all, it was really only very tiny and —

Hang on, Deet – here we go!

FLASH.

The glaring whiteness dwindled to be a speck like all the others. I marked it for future reference. In case we wanted to come back to it later.

A wash of bright stretched from one infinity to the other. All the yesterdays stacked against all the tomorrows. The thing had a structure, but I was too close to it to see what it was. I'd have to move back – and the greater darkness backdrop was still just as far away and —

'Deet! Can't we stop and rest for just a minute?'

'Oh, no, kitten! Come on, we're almost there! This it it! This is really it!'

And —

FLASH!

I grabbed her hand and we went. Yeah, this *was* it! I didn't have to say it anymore. It wasn't necessary. I was convinced – because it really *was* it. *IT! The* trip – and it was still going!

A great wheel of spiraling sparkling dust turning against the ultimate velvet. Turning, turning. Oh wow, how big is that thing? How big?

FLASH!

Tiny – really very tiny. A myriad of them spin twinkly through the darkness. Like snowflakes, scattering in a wind, roiling ever outward. We dive back into and out of it. I want to keep going. Expand to fill the whole —

FLASH!

– little fireflies disappear into the hole. And —

FLASH!

FLASH!

FLASH!

And I still hadn't filled it.

FLASH!

But I was getting there! I was!

FLASH!

Oh, Woozle? Isn't this the greatest —

FLASH!

Almost, almost. Just once more, I think – and then we'll fill this tiny black cubicle, and then one more after that and we'll burst it and look down onto it from the outside and look down at all the row upon row of identical shiny black globes and —

FLASH!

Not yet!

FLASH!

Still not yet! Dammit! Once more. I want it, dammit! Let's go, Woozle. Once more.

FLASH!

And I throw my hands outstretched into the never-more, always reaching and grasping, that elusive black wall remaining just ever so out of my reach and —

FLASH!

FLASH!

FLASH! DAMMIT!

Blackness, nothing but blackness and blackness beyond. Almost, almost. I almost made it, this time I almost made it . . .

FLASH!

But nothing.

Okay, so we don't do the big number this time around. We dive back into the wrong end of the microscope and shrink down into the other direction of infinity – inwardly.

Ping.

The little wheels reappear, spinning madly. I pick one at random and down we go, and –

Ping.

– it becomes a big wheel. I head for a spiral arm, zig-zag around the exploding core, and –

Ping.

– pop out at a *here* in the middle of empty brightness. Rocky nothingnesses whirl about it. The wrong one. Not mine. Try again. So —

Ping.

And this time, *here* is a blue and red binary, a pinpoint of bright and a bloated crimson vagueness. Streamers of blood-colored gas spiral outward from the giant. The lesser-sized one would have been lost among them if not for its brilliance. But — This one isn't mine either.

Ping.

Up and out again. An explosion, a never-ending one. Dazzling, sleeting, brighting, sheeting, flaring, flashing, glaring, shimmering, slashing intensity of light so thick you have to push at it to move. All around me. All around. We hung at the core of the supernova and —

FLASHED!

The wheel again, the great wheel. No, that's the wrong direction. I wanted to go the other way. My God, how big is that thing anyway? Immense. No, tiny – tiny, tiny, remember! I am immense. Remember the outer blackness, how big it is and how big I am and never fill it. That wheel is only a mote of dust in the hungry sucking dark. I am as big to the wheel as it is to me. I am small and vast and —

Ping.

I remember and dive back into it. Back to the home world, right Woozle?

Woozle?

Hey, Woozle – where are you?

Woozle . . . ?

I'm alone in the vampire dark. Somewhere I've lost my —

'Woozle!!'

No answer.

I plunge through the night, carefully retracing. Where did I leave her? Where did I let go? She was with me here. Flash. Here. Flash. Here.

She was with me all the way. Or was she? She wasn't. She wasn't with me at all.

Flash/Ping.

Back down into the wheel. Back down. Home system, home sun, home planet. Yeah, that's it. Blue-white streaked disk. Dive into it.

I know what must have happened. She couldn't keep up. Yeah, that's right. She couldn't keep up. So she went home without me. She went on home. Yeah, that's what she must have done. Yeah, that's it. She wouldn't just run off on her own.

Into the disk and down the long tunnel and the walls unstretch, become a room again, and I land on the floor and down.

The room is empty. And alone.
All of them were empty —